COGNIZANCE

Published by Pugnacious Publishing

COGNIZANCE

Guy Portman

ONE

RAT HAS BEEN CHASING MY BUS. The driver just kicked me off because I was laughing so much. Thought Rat had disappeared, as couldn't see him through the upper deck's rear window. When I step off the bus, I see him in the distance.

'DEVIL CUNT!'

He is approximately fifty metres away and heading straight for me. As the bus drives off, the people on the pavement stare at Rat. I don't want to run away from him, so I remain at the bus stop. He'll be out of breath from all that running. A couple of solid punches to the body and he'll be done. I slip my mini rucksack off my shoulder, set it on the ground, and raise my hands. Rat's here. He is breathing hard and his face is red. He lashes out at me with his right foot. I pull my leg back; the kick doesn't touch me. Rat grabs my collar with his left hand. I bend my knees and hit him with a short right cross to the chest. He makes a wheezing noise but doesn't release his grip. Rat throws a hook with his spare hand. I block it with my left forearm, bring my head forward and butt him on the bridge of the nose.

He releases his grip, stumbles backwards, then lunges at me. A big black man grabs him from behind by the waist. Rat is frantically flailing his arms and legs about. The man is muscular, might be a body builder, and there is no way that skinny, puny loser is breaking free. The man is telling Rat to calm down. He's not though, he's snarling and trying to break free. This is hilarious.

'Ha ha ha.'

People have gathered by the bus stop. Rat spits a mouthful of phlegm at me. I jump backwards; it lands on the ground by my feet. Disgusting. Some of the people are saying they'll phone the police if he doesn't stop freaking out. Want to stay and see what happens. But then Rat screeches, 'MURDERER!'

The people are looking at me. It is time to go. I pick up my mini rucksack, sling it over my shoulder, and quickly walk off. He is still screeching *murderer* and other stuff. So, he suspects I killed his best friend, probably only friend, Mum's ex-partner, Fool's Gold. However, he doesn't have any evidence, and no one is going to believe the moron. It's a fair walk to my aunt's flat from here. She's got cancer, is in hospital, and doesn't have long to live. Staying in her flat, as our house is rented out because me and Mum were living in Antigua. Mum returned to London when her sister got cancer. She made me come back. I was only over there for one term ... Have just arrived at the flat. Mum is in the kitchen folding clothes.

'Hey, how was Serena?'

'She's fine.' *Was at her house earlier.* 'About to go to Singapore.'

Mum folds one of my T-shirts, puts it on top of a pile of clothes, and says, 'Her father's living out there, right?'

'Yeah.'

'How was her mother?'

'Seemed fine.'

'She is nice and has been good to you.' Mum stops folding clothes and looks at me. Her eyes are puffy. 'You must have been shocked to see your aunt in that state.' *I went to the hospital before going to Serena's.* '*Hhh*, she's looking so ill. Lost so much weight.'

True. She used to be fat, that's why I call her Aunt Fatso.

Could rename her Aunt Thin-so. Doesn't have the same ring to it though. Mum is folding more clothes. I go into my bedroom and take from the mini rucksack the two hundred pounds I got changed at the bureau de change after I went to Serena's house. Earned it selling drugs in Antigua. The money is stuffed in a rolled-up pair of socks at the back of the sock drawer in the chest of drawers. Still got five hundred pounds worth of Eastern Caribbean Dollars. Didn't want to change it all at once, as it would look suspicious because I'm young and they might wonder where the money came from.

When we were in Antigua, Mum said she'd find my father's death certificate when we returned to London. I reminded her on the way here from the airport. That was two days ago. And she still hasn't found it. Aunt Fatso is staring at me from on top of the chest of drawers. It looks as if she's about to tell me off. Bossy that woman is. Will soon be was. I turn the framed photograph around, so it is facing the wall.

'Horatio!' I go to the kitchen. 'Shaneeka will be here in an hour.' *My sister is visiting from college.* 'Think you should give her your room and you sleep on the sofa in the living room.' *Typical.* 'She'd appreciate it. Strip your bed and put the bedding behind the sofa for now. I'll make the bed up for her.'

'Mum?'

'Yes.'

'Have you found my father's death certificate?'

Mum *huffs*, and says, 'No, not yet, haven't had a chance.'

'You said you would—'

'And I will! Give me a chance. Got a lot on at the moment what with my sister being so ill. You'll just have to wait. Patience is a virtue.'

She better get a move on. I return to the bedroom and use the iPad. There is an email from my Antiguan girlfriend Dalilah. She wishes I was there. Mum is calling me.

'What?'

'Have you stripped the bed yet …? Horatio, answer me!'

Ahh!

Fifty minutes later – Brrrnnnggg. That was the doorbell. Mum tells me to come out of my room. I do. In the hallway, she says, 'You haven't seen your sister in months. Be pleased to see her.'

Brrr— Mum presses the entry button on the intercom and opens the door. Can hear running footsteps coming up the stairs. It's her. She says, '*Hi.*' She hugs Mum around the neck, then does the same to me. 'Brother, long time no see.' She takes a step back. 'Think you've grown a bit.'

'He has.'

Mum nudges me in the side with her elbow. I say, 'Hi.'

We all go into the living room. Mum says, 'It's lovely to have both my children with me.' She puts an arm over my sister's shoulders and her other arm over mine. 'Do you two want a drink? There's Coca-Cola in the fridge.'

I say, 'Yeah.'

My sister says, 'Yes please.'

Mum says, 'Horatio, help me with the drinks.'

I follow her into the kitchen. She pushes the door closed, places her fists on her hips, and hisses, 'What do you think you're doing? You've said only one word to her.' She prods me in the chest. 'You're going to tell her about Antigua. Oh, and you can start off by saying you like her hair. It's been cut short and highlighted.'

Mum pours Coca-Cola into three glasses. I take two of them through to the living room, pass one to my sister, and say, 'I like your hair.'

'Thank you. Tell me all about Antigua?'

'It was alright by and large. My school was quite good. Facilities sucked, but the teaching wasn't bad.'

Mum comes into the living room. We talk about Antigua, but not for long because they change the subject to Aunt Fatso. At dinner she is all they discuss. We eat marinated chicken breasts and broccoli. I am now having dessert – a pot of chocolate mousse. My sister and Mum are going to watch *Love Island.* There is no way I'm watching that rubbish. After clearing up, Mum goes to her room and my sister goes to the living room and switches the television on. Think I'll read in the kitchen until *Love Island* is over and I can have the living room to myself. Mum comes into the kitchen holding a piece of paper.

'Here's what you wanted.'

She puts the piece of paper on the table and leaves. I turn it over. At the top is a coat of arms and the words Certified Copy Of An Entry. Below that in capital letters is – DEATH. There's a table below it. It has my father's name – Dyson Devereux. His gender, the date of his death, the registration district, the sub-district, his date of birth, occupation, and usual address. At the bottom is the cause of death. Homicide by shooting.

So, here it is: the death certificate Mum has been hiding from me all these years. She should have shown me this when I was young. He died when I was five. That was nearly a decade ago. Mum finally told me the truth about what happened to him in Antigua. Before that she just said he had disappeared. I hold the certificate up and read through it several times. My father was forty when he died. He was born in Dorset. Think Dorset is in the southwest. I look the county up on the internet. It is in the southwest; it's on the coast. Why did he move to London? Was it because of his work, or did he study here too?

I am still looking at the certificate when Mum walks into the kitchen and tells me *Love Island* has finished. In the living room, I read and watch television. But I can't focus on either, as keep thinking about my father. How did he end up getting killed? Found a few articles on the internet when I was in Antigua. They didn't have much information though. He was found dead in a flat not far from here along with a dead Albanian man and a dead Moldovan woman. The police thought my father and the Albanian shot each other, and the Moldovan was shot by the

Albanian. My father had an important job; he was head of a department at a local council. Why was my father in that flat? What was he involved in? Was he a secret agent? Involved in organised crime?

*

The next morning – I awaken on my side on the sofa feeling stiff. It's 08:16. Feeling tired, as couldn't get to sleep for ages because I was thinking about my father. I get up, fold up the duvet, stuff it behind the sofa, dump my pillow on top of it, and put on the clothes I was wearing yesterday. Will change into clean ones after breakfast. They are in the kitchen. Mum and my sister say, 'Good morning.'

I say, 'Good morning,' sit down at the table, take a piece of toast from the plate in the middle of the table, and spread butter and marmalade on it.

Mum says, 'We're leaving for the hospital in half an hour. Have your breakfast and get ready.'

Ahh! Don't want to go to the hospital again. Was there yesterday. 'Mum, I went to the hospital yesterday.'

'You're coming, end of. We're going to put on a united front.'

I have a bite of toast. They are talking about Aunt Fatso. Practically all they discuss now. Week after next, I'm starting a new school. It's the same school Mum was planning to send me to after I was expelled from my old one for stabbing a boy in the hand with scissors in art class. His fault; not mine. Then Mum changed our plans and we moved to Antigua. Now I'm back. My new school is a shithole. Would far rather return to the school I was expelled from, or my school in Antigua.

Burrr, burrr – someone's phone is ringing. Mum stands up, takes her phone off a counter, and answers it. I pour orange juice into a glass. Mum says, 'Now's fine, we've just finished breakfast ... Do hope the boiler's not on the blink. Could do without that.' *She's probably talking to her tenants.* 'It's being serviced soon. Fingers crossed ...' I have a gulp of orange juice. 'Oh, really! What did he look like ...? White guy. Tall, thin, long nose.' *Rat.* She taps the fingertips of her left hand on the counter. 'No idea who that could be. Let me know if he poles up again. Thanks for letting me know ... Bye.'

Mum puts the phone down and crosses her arms. My sister says, 'Mum, something up?'

'It was one of our tenants on the phone. A man's been loitering near the house, acting suspiciously.'

My sister sits up straight, and says, 'Really?'

'Yeah. Probably nothing to worry about.'

Fits his description exactly. So, he is hanging around near my house. Because he ran into me yesterday, he must think I'm living there. In a month's time, I will be.

*

09:35 – They are beside the bed; I am standing behind them. My sister is holding Aunt Fatso's hand while Mum rearranges her blanket. My sister says, 'Back to college today. It's still the holidays for another week. Have quite a lot going on there though, so I'm going today. Promise I will come and see you soon.'

Aunt Fatso murmurs, 'Thank you, darling.' Her voice is so weak can barely hear her. Used to be loud and bossy, especially when she was talking to me. 'You've been a godsend to me.'

'And to me,' says Mum. 'What with me being in Antigua, it was a relief knowing Shaneeka was here for you.'

Mum strokes my sister's arm. Next to me there is a wheeled table. On it there is a carton of Lindt Lindor milk chocolate truffles. It was here yesterday; I ate two of them. No more have been eaten. She sure is ill. Before the cancer, she would have gobbled the entire carton in no time. I stick my hand in the carton, take out a milk chocolate truffle, unwrap it, and pop it into my mouth. A bit rich for this early in the morning. More of a teatime thing these Lindt chocolate truffles.

'Hhh.' That is Mum sobbing. 'Hhh ...'

My sister rests her head on Mum's shoulder. I help myself to another chocolate truffle. While chewing it, I think about Rat. Must've been him the tenant saw. Too much of a coincidence otherwise for there to be a tall, thin man with a long nose loitering by the house. He went berserk yesterday and is obviously completely mad. What is he planning to do next? If it comes down to it, I will take him out with a boxing combo. Don't want him making those murder accusations around Mum. Rat doesn't have any evidence, and it wouldn't be the end of the world. Would rather he didn't though; it wouldn't be helpful.

My sister is bent over the bed hugging my aunt. Mum comes over to me, grips my arm, leans into me, and hisses in my ear, 'What're you doing?'

Eating Lindt milk chocolate truffles is what. Mum tugs my arm; I shuffle forward. She is even greyer and gaunter than yesterday. Must be near death.

*

Sixteen days later – I get off the bus. There are loads of pupils from my school on the pavement. One of them is a tall mixed-race boy from my year. Someone told me he knows where to score skunk. Decent amounts, ounces, not the ten quid baggies the gang sell at school. He's smoking skunk, can smell it from here. Outside the school, there is a wall with graffiti on it. There are two spray-painted gang logos. One is a red circle with a knife in the middle and *DAGGERZ* sprayed below it. Next to it in green paint is – *C CREW*. The first C has a crown above it. Red paint has been sprayed over *C CREW*. Last Wednesday, I saw someone from the council removing the gang graffiti from this wall. Didn't take long for them to re-spray it. These two logos have been sprayed on the glass at the bus stop too. Daggerz are the gang from school; C Crew are a rival gang.

It's incredibly noisy in the corridors as usual. Pupils shouting, laughing, swearing. This is by far the noisiest school I've been to, and the worst by a longshot. Must be one of the shittest schools in Greater London. If my father was still alive, he definitely wouldn't have sent me here. First class of the day is English. The classroom is nearly as noisy as the corridors. There are thirty pupils in the classes here, which is way too many. Some of them will bunk off, they always do. It's usually close to thirty though. I choose a desk in a middle row, as far away from the biggest idiots as possible. The teacher comes in and puts her stuff on the table at the front of the classroom.

'Quieten down, please.' Half the class continue talking. 'Quieten down, I said. And go to your desks!'

Some of them are still talking. In Antigua, the moment the teacher walked into the classroom, everyone stopped talking. That all-boys school was a bit of a shithole too. The boys though were well behaved. Here half the boys are unruly, and some of the girls are even worse. The teacher is summarising the first two chapters of *Jane Eyre*. I take my phone from my trouser pocket, hold it under my desk and look at some algebra questions on the algebra app I downloaded last week. These advanced algebra questions are more challenging than anything I'll be facing in my GCSEs next year. The teacher is reading from chapter three of *Jane Eyre*.

'The next thing I remember is, waking up with a feeling as if I had had a frightful nightmare, and seeing before me a terrible red glare, crossed with thick black bars. I heard voices, too, speaking with a hollow sound, and as if muffled by a rush of wind or water ...' There is whispering going on, giggling too. 'I knew quite well that I was in my own bed, and that the red glare was the nursery fire. It was night: a candle burnt on the table ...'

The teacher asks a girl two desks in front of me to continue reading. She stands up and reads. The girl is a refugee from Darfur. She told the class the other day that English is her third language after Dinka and Arabic. Her reading level though is higher than some of the native speakers here, including the imbecile picking his nose at a desk three to my left. Dalton has a D shaved into the hair on the side of his head. Can see it from here. He is the little brother of the head of the Daggerz gang. The teacher won't be asking Dalton to read that's for sure. He has the reading age of a five-year-old. I call him Dunce. Have a multiple-choice test here. First question. *Which of the following expressions has the smallest value when a=5 and b=-3?* Easy. Answer is *b–4a*. Next. Child's play these. The gang sell weed at school and don't allow anyone else to. There are four members of the gang in my class – three boys and a girl.

I am in the last class of the day, geography. In the rear row of desks, a group of girls are talking non-stop. The teacher is explaining how the word relief refers to the way landscapes change in height. This is the first thing I've learnt at this school. Time to crack open the champagne. At a desk to my left, Tricia is blowing gum. The bubble bursts. She sucks the gum into her mouth and chews on it. That girl spends as much time chewing gum, as cows do chewing grass. Tricia is a member of the Daggerz gang. She has a sister in the sixth form who also is. Tricia's noticed me looking at her and is waving at me. *Ah!* Dunce is leaning across the aisle and tugging on Tricia's arm. Now he's glaring at me. Idiot.

The teacher is prodding at upland areas on a map of England. The areas are The Pennines, Lake District, Dartmoor, and Exmoor. The highest mountain in England is in the Lake District. Scafell Pike is nine hundred and seventy-eight metres above sea level. That isn't very high. My phone beeps. I take it out and look at it under the desk. A text from Serena. Tricia isn't the only blonde trying to get my attention. Serena is ten times hotter than Tricia.

Today, Now

Hi Gorgeous, School is so boring 😪
Craving 🚬😌💨🚗🔒 School is dry. 🆘💔

School is finished for the day. I leave the classroom, go along the corridor, weave past pupils spewing from a classroom, and enter the hallway. Dunce's big brother Darragh brushes past me. He is built like a rugby prop or an NFL player. Has no neck, must weigh eighteen stone, and like his little brother he has a smudged nose. Darragh is in the lower sixth and has one more year left after this one. Darragh slaps a boy on the shoulder, and says, 'Oi, oi.'

The boy who can get the skunk is standing on the pavement. Stands out like a sore thumb does Bart, as he's a head taller than virtually everyone else. NBA height he is, and he still has a year or two of growing yet. I jog over to him, and say, 'Wait up.'

'What's up?'

'Want to get some skunk.'

'Keep your voice down.' He glances over his shoulder and crosses the road. I follow him. Doesn't say anything until we go around the corner. 'What're you talking about?'

'An ounce of skunk. How much is it?'

'Don't know.' He holds his hands up at shoulder level. 'Why're you asking me?'

'Someone told me you know where to get it.'

'Did they now?'

'Yeah.'

'Don't believe rumours.' He prods my shoulder. 'You could get me in big shit just saying that.'

'Can you get some for me, or not?'

‘I barely know you.’ His eyes narrow. ‘Spoken to you like twice. Ask me again in a month or so.’

‘I need some ASAP.’

‘Can’t help you.’ He holds his hands up at shoulder height. ‘That’s all I’ve got to say.’

Damn, it didn’t go as planned.

TWO

THE FOLLOWING MONTH – There are no parking spaces by our house. Mum sighs, and says, 'A nightmare this.'

It's a Saturday is why. Most of our neighbours are at home. There is a space on the other side of the street. While Mum parks, I look out of the window. No sign of Rat. The tenants left yesterday. Mum had the house professionally cleaned this morning. This is the third trip back and forth from the flat with our stuff. And fortunately, it's the last. Tight squeeze this space is. Earlier, I asked Mum if the man her tenant saw was still hanging around. She said they hadn't mentioned him. Rat probably realised I was living elsewhere and buggered off. With any luck permanently. My sister says, 'Parking skills Mum.'

'Right,' says Mum. 'Let's get this over with.'

My sister opens the boot and I pull from it two wheeled suitcases. Mum grabs their handles and drags them across the road to our house. I close the boot. My sister takes a cardboard box off the backseat.

'Taking the light one. Heavy one's yours.'

Mine has kitchen stuff in it. She waits for a car to pass then lugs the box across the road. My sister is here for the weekend to help and visit Aunt Fatso in the hospital. Should make that Aunt Ex-Fatso. Ex because she's not fat anymore. Soon it will be Ex-Aunt Fatso because she'll be dead. There's no way I'm going to the hospital with them, not after all this moving. I want to relax. Mum is crossing the road.

'What're you waiting for? Carry that box in. Chop, chop.'

I pick up the box and cross the road. Other than the stint in Antigua and the month I've just spent at my aunt's house, been living here since I was a baby. I carry the box through the hallway and into the kitchen. Spick and span in here, those cleaners did a good job. How's my room looking? I hurtle upstairs. The bed has been pulled away from the wall, but other than that it's as I left it. My stuff is on the floor in that suitcase, mini rucksack, and cardboard box. Protruding from the top of the box is the handle of the mini cricket bat my father gave me when I was five. A storage company has the rest of my stuff. It should be delivered soon.

I go downstairs. Can hear Mum and my sister talking in the kitchen. I open the living room door and step inside. Popped my head in here earlier. The furniture has been moved. Before the sofa was directly in front of me, facing the television. But now it is by the far wall facing the middle of the room. It was on that sofa I killed him – Mum's boyfriend, Fool's Gold. I had put ground-up sleeping pills in his beer and he was passed out.

His trousers and boxer shorts were around his ankles and his head was drooped forward onto his chest. Could clearly see his bald patch. I had looped a belt over his neck, which was attached by a cord to the metal handle on the window at the rear of the room. On the floor by his feet there were two empty beer cans, and on the sofa next to him the box of tissues and packet of Viagra I put there. On the coffee table in front of him, his phone was propped up on four DVD boxes – *American Psycho*, *Casino*, *Goodfellas*, *Texas Chainsaw Massacre*. On the phone, an erotic asphyxiation porn video was playing on a loop. The coffee table is in the far corner now. Right, let's put everything as it should be. I pick up the coffee table and put it down where it was before, in front of the television. Then I lift up one end of the sofa and drag it across the floor. Mum comes in.

'What the hell are you doing?'

'Moving the furniture to where it was before. Where it's meant to be.'

'No! Put the sofa and coffee table back.'

'But Mum.'

'Now!'

What's her problem? My sister runs into the room and says, 'What's going on? Why're you shouting?'

Mum shakes her head really fast, and says, 'It doesn't matter, darling. It's, ah, under control.'

They both watch me as I drag the sofa over to the far wall. And they continue watching as I carry the coffee table to the far corner ... I am in my room at my desk, studying the periodic table on the iPad. In the exam next year, I'll be provided with a copy of the periodic table. But the teacher said the more familiar we are with it, the better. Already know it pretty well. And will be an expert soon enough. There are six alkali metals in the periodic table. Lithium, sodium, potassium, rubidium, caesium, francium. There are also six metalloids. Boron, silicon, germanium, arsenic, antimony, tellurium. There is a knock on my door.

'Come in.' The door opens. It's Mum. 'Yeah.'

'We're going to the hospital ...'

The door closes. While they're out, I'll move the furniture in the living room to the correct position. Will move it back before they return.

*

Two days later – It's the last class of the day. The chemistry teacher is attempting to explain the periodic table to the class. He's not going to succeed though. For starters, four pupils including Dunce bunked this class to smoke weed and do nitrous oxide. Heard them talking about it in the last class, biology. Half of those here are either playing with their phones under their desks or talking to each other. The boy on my right is fast asleep and the girl on my left looks mega stoned. Superimposed on a screen at the front of the classroom is the periodic table. Has the symbols on it but not the names.

'There are nine post-transition metals. *Al* stands for aluminium. The other commonly used element in this category is this.' The teacher taps the periodic table with his ruler. 'Can anyone tell me what *Pb* stands for?' *Lead.* I raise my arm. The Bangladeshi girl has her arm raised, as does the Dinka refugee from Darfur. The teacher asks the Dinka. She gives the correct answer. 'Can anyone name any of the other post-transition metals?' I raise my arm again. He points at me. 'Yes.'

'*Po* is polonium. It's highly radioactive and has no stable isotopes.'

'I'm impressed. Can't say the same for most of the rest of you.'

The bell goes and everyone races for the door. Except me, the Bangladeshi, the Dinka, and a boy with crooked legs who can't walk properly. The Dinka says to me, 'Horatio, you seen this app for the periodic table?' She shows me her iPhone. It has the periodic table on the screen. 'You can select what you want to view and what you want to test yourself on. Look.' The names have all disappeared and there are only symbols. 'Can test yourself this way. Or only display the names. It has questions too.'

'That's pretty good. Will get it for my Samsung Galaxy.'

She gives me the name of the app. As I walk along the corridors, I look for the app in the app store. Rubbish, they don't have it for Samsung Galaxy. In the hallway, I hear shouting coming from outside. I go outside. A posse of youths wearing green tracksuits have gathered on the pavement. Must be the rival gang, the C-Crew from the council estate near here. Pupils are shouting and swearing at them. Several dart off, probably to look for Darragh. A girl from the C-Crew is spraying the gang's sign in green paint on the wall outside the school. A boy and a girl from my school rush over and grab her. C-Crew gang members pull them off then form a semi-circle in front of the girl, who resumes spraying the wall. Darragh is marching from the direction of the bus stop. A dozen pupils are following behind him including his little brother. Darragh bellows, 'COME ON YOU CUNTS!'

Darragh marches over to the rival gang and butts heads with the tallest of them. He must be the gang's leader. They are pushing their foreheads against each other like battling rams. The C-Crew gang leader is being pushed across the pavement. The gang members are screaming, swearing, shouting, and throwing up gang signs. Daggerz's is the little finger of the right hand held horizontally at the bottom of the left index finger. C-Crew's is a C shape made with the left index finger and thumb. The gang leaders have stopped butting heads and are snarling at each other. The C-Crew members position themselves behind their leader. Thirty or so pupils gather behind Darragh. Teaching staff are hurrying out of the school. And the headmaster's here. He shouts, 'Away with you lot, or I'm phoning the police!'

The female French teacher grabs Darragh by the waist and another teacher grips his sleeve. The C-Crew tear off down the pavement, swearing and throwing up gang signs as they go. Darragh is surrounded by a circle of teachers. He holds his hands up, and says, 'Relax, I'm calm.'

The headmaster is talking with Darragh outside the entrance. Darragh nods and walks off. The French teacher and another teacher accompany him. He'll be heading for the bus stop. Same way I'm going. My phone beeps. It's a text.

....

Today, Now

Get yourself to the hospital, right away. Don't dawdle.
Mum X

....

Ahh! Sick of that place. Been at school all day and want some time on my own. What's so important that I have to be there. Could Aunt Fatso be on her way out? When I arrive at the bus stop, Darragh is boarding a bus with some other pupils. The bus drives off and the teachers who were escorting him cross the road.

My bus is here. It's packed, there are no seats, and it's noisy. I look out of the window. It's raining. Good weather never seems to stick around for long in London. When I get off the bus, it's still raining. I jog along the crowded pavements. By the time I reach the hospital my hair is wet and I'm a little out of breath. A nurse comes with me to the room, knocks on the door, and opens it. I go inside. Mum is sitting beside the bed with her head in her hands, making whimpering noises.

'H-hhh …' She grabs my wrist. 'Well done getting here so quickly.' Aunt Fatso is lying on her back in the bed with her head tilted to one side. Her face is a grey colour, her eyes are closed, and her chest is heaving slowly up and down. Mum is still squeezing my wrist. Why did she say I had to come here? Mum stops whimpering and wipes her eyes with her forearm. 'Come outside for a sec.' We leave the room. In the corridor, she says in a hushed voiced, 'Tanice hasn't got long. Think this, a-hh, will be the last time you, a-hh, see her. She's, ah, not conscious, she's in a coma.' Mum strokes my arm. 'I'm so sorry.' *For what?* She stops stroking my arm, looks up at the ceiling, and takes a big intake of air through her nose. 'Right, a-hh, I need to pull it together and go and speak to the doctor. Go in and talk to her.' She grips my wrist. 'Maybe, a-hh, it would be nice if you told her about some nice memories you have of spending time with her. Okay?'

What nice memories? Mum wipes her wet cheeks with her forearm, breathes rapidly in and out, then pushes her palm into my lower back. I go into the room and pull the door shut. She is in exactly the same position as before. I stand beside the bed and look down at her.

'So, this is it, you're dying. Probably only a day or two left.

You're only the third dying person I've seen. Strange thing is they've all been fairly recently. First was Brandon. I called him Fool's Gold. You seemed a bit suspicious, as I was the only person in the house when he died. I did kill him. Strangled him while he was passed out.' Her eyelids flicker. 'Ha, made it look like he'd died while jerking off to erotic asphyxiation pornography. Nice touch that. Second dying person was a drug dealer I killed in Antigua. After I shot him the first time, he crawled across the floor. I shot him two more times in the head.'

Could stuff a pillow over her face, finish her off, and make her kill number three. Might look a bit suspicious though when Mum comes in and finds her sister dead. There is a new box of Lindt Lindor milk chocolate truffles on the table. Wonder who brought these. I take one out of the carton, unwrap it, and pop it in my mouth.

'These Lindt Lindor chocolate truffles are good. Sickly though. You were a big chocolate fan.' Her eyelids are flickering. 'Will never forget how quickly you could get through a large bag of Maltesers. You'd grab whole handfuls of them and stuff them in your gob. You'd do it in your car, in your flat, all over the place. Quite a sight it was.'

The door opens, Mum comes into the room, and says, 'How're you two getting along?'

'Fine. I'm going to grab a bite.'

'Sure, see you in a bit. Shaneeka's on her way.'

I go to the ground floor. There is a cafeteria down here. I get a ham and cheese sandwich and a can of Coca-Cola, sit at a table, and use the algebra app on my phone. Been here half an hour when my sister runs past. She's seen me. She slides to a halt, pivots, and comes over to me. Her eyes are wide open.

'What're you doing here?'

'Doing some algebra on my phone.'

She huffs and races off.

*

The following afternoon – School has just ended for the day. I cross the road and turn the corner. The tall mixed-race boy from my class, Bart, is waiting for me. He has a gym bag slung over his shoulder.

'Got the dough, yeah?'

'Of course.'

'Two-twenty.'

'Yes.'

I have two hundred and twenty pounds with me. We walk off. Will sell the skunk at ten quid a gramme. That's a sixty quid profit. Well, might smoke a bit with Serena. Only a gramme or two though. The profit margin isn't great unlike the cocaine in Antigua. But it's something to keep me ticking over. Diagonally in front of us and to the left, is a high-rise council block. Bart stops, slips the gym bag off his shoulder, takes off his school blazer, stuffs it in the bag, and says, 'Take yours off. School badge is a red rag to a bull in there. You get me?'

I take off my blazer, fold it and stick it in my left armpit. Surrounding the council estate is a low wall with the C-Crew's logo sprayed all over it. On the pavement two girls from my school are taking off their school blazers. They are wearing hijabs. Seems unlikely they're here to score drugs. Presumably they live on this estate. And they don't even dare wear their school blazers.

'Before we go any further bruv, be clear on the rules. The weed is for home, not school. It's not to be on school premises.' He prods me in the chest. 'Get caught with it at school, got nought to do with me. You get me?'

'Yeah.'

He clicks his fingers and says, 'Give me the dough!'

There's no way I'm handing him that much money.

'I'm coming in with you.'

He *tuts* and says, 'Alright. Don't fuck up in there.'

Next to the entrance to the council block there is an intercom. He presses a button on it. Someone answers. He speaks into it. The door opens and we go in. The interior is made of yellow concrete. C-Crew has been sprayed on the floor. We go into a lift smelling of piss and ascend to the top floor, the fifteenth floor. He taps five times on the door of a flat at the end of the corridor. We are let in by a girl wearing a shiny green tracksuit. Stinks of skunk in here. We follow her into a tiny living room with a filthy carpet and a massive television. The tall skinny gang leader who was butting heads with Darragh is slouched on a chair smoking a joint. Two teenage boys and a girl are sitting on a sofa opposite him. They are all wearing green tracksuits. Evidently, this is the C-Crew's uniform. The gang's boss juts his chin at me.

'You from that shit school?'

'Yes.'

'Not one of them Daggerz faggots, are yah?'

'He's not,' says Bart. 'Can vouch for him.'

'Weren't asking you.'

'No,' I say. 'Certainly not.'

'What you after?'

'An ounce.'

'Two-twenty.' He blows a smoke ring. 'Cough it up.' I get the money out of my mini rucksack. He tells the girl to count it. She does, twice. She then passes a twenty-pound note to Bart. A boy gets off the sofa, takes a polythene-wrapped lump of skunk and throws it at me. I catch it one handed. Looks about right. 'Daggerz are pussies. Faggot Darragh was pissing himself when I showed up.' *That's a lie.* 'Will fuck him up next time.' This idiot is in his early twenties, and he's a lot taller than Darragh. Could be six four maybe more. But he's thin and looks puny. Darragh would rip him to pieces. When they were butting heads, it was obvious who was stronger. 'What you waiting for? Get the fuck aht. Wankers!'

*

17:53 – Mum has returned from the hospital. Aunt Fatso isn't dead yet. There is a knock on my door.

'Yeah.'

Mum steps into the room, and says, 'Don't think Tanice has long. Surprised she's still hanging on. Can't be more than a day or two. A-hh, oh, I heard back about my interview.' *Mum had an interview last week.* 'Will be returning to the council in two weeks. The same department I was working in before but a different job. Hhh, work is the last thing on my mind right now. Horatio!'

'Yes.'

'Turn around and look at me.' I swivel my chair so it is facing her. 'How was your day?'

'Not too bad, I suppose. Don't like my school though. It's rubbish. Barely learning anything new.'

'Shouldn't have got expelled from your last school then, should you? If you hadn't, you could have returned there.'

'It wasn't my fault.'

She plants her fists on her hips, and says, 'Don't start that again.'

'But Mum—'

'Enough! This isn't the time. If you hadn't noticed, my sister is dying.' She removes her fists from her hips and blows air from her mouth. 'Ah, got something for you. The rest of our stuff was delivered from storage this morning. Wait there.' She reappears with a large cardboard box. 'Here you are.'

'My stuff isn't in that box; it's in a different one.'

She puts the box on the floor, and says, 'Some of your father's things are in here.' I jump off the chair, grab the box, dump it on the desk, and rip the tape off it. 'Been holding on to them for you. You're old enough to have them now.' Inside there is a navy-blue jacket and trousers. It's a suit; a nice suit. I hold the jacket up against my front. 'Suits you. And it nearly fits. You're almost the same height as him. He was near on six foot.' I set the suit down on the bed, reach into the box and pull out a tie. It's a black, shiny tie. Feels like scales. It's snakeskin, must be. I hold it up to my throat. 'Remember that tie. It brings back memories. He was always the smartest dressed man by a country mile at the council we worked at.' *Sniff.* 'Well, I'll leave you to it. Will give you a shout when dinner's ready.'

Mum leaves. There is another suit – dark grey. It's thicker than the blue suit. I like it. There are three more ties in here. A green tie, a blue tie, and this stylish, lilac silk tie from Forzieri. And there are some handkerchiefs too. This pink handkerchief could be stuffed in the breast pocket of the blue suit. At the bottom of the box there are two books. I pull one out. It's a Latin dictionary. Know my father liked Latin because he bought me some Latin language learning DVDs. Was too young to remember him giving them to me. But Mum told me he did. Don't know where they are now. The other book is a novel – *Bleak House* by Charles Dickens. For school, we're meant to read a novel each term in our free time. I'll be reading this. And at Aunt Fatso's funeral, I'll be wearing the black snakeskin tie and one of these suits.

*

08:43 – The next morning – I'm on the bus. In the seat in front of me, a boy from my school is complaining to the girl sitting next to him that the Daggerz gang only have hash *at the mo*, and he wants green. I lean forward and tell him I can spare a little bit. Most of the skunk will probably be flogged to Serena's friends, but am keeping a couple of grammes on me in case anyone wants some. He is whispering with the girl. On the way off the bus, he says, 'Want a tenner's worth.'

'Fine.'

We go into an alleyway behind the bus stop. The girl follows us. I take a transparent seal bag containing one gramme from my trouser pocket. I open the bag, he sniffs it, and says, 'Alright.'

I'm passing him the drugs and he's passing me the money

when I notice the girl is holding her phone out towards us. Is she taking a photograph? I say, 'What're you doing?'

'Nothing. Looking at my phone is all.'

When I approach her, she scampers off. I make my way to school.

An hour later – We are studying ratios. Basic stuff this. I am far too advanced for it. This crap school is holding me back. If my father was still alive, I would be at a good school like the one Serena goes to now. She was at my old school, which was pretty decent. Now she's at a private all-girls day school. If Aunt Fatso leaves Mum money maybe I can change schools. She has, soon-to-be had, a few quid. And there's her flat. On the whiteboard the teacher writes, *A piece of wood is forty-five centimetres long. The length is divided in the ratio 7:2. Work out the length of each part.* Easy. Seven plus two equals nine parts. Forty-five divided by nine equals five. Seven times five equals thirty-five and two times five equals ten. Pre-school maths this.

Dunce is grinning at me. He has nothing to grin about; he is incapable of working out the lengths. I take *Bleak House* from my mini rucksack and read it under the desk. *Fog everywhere. Fog up the river, where it flows among green aits.* I look up what *ait* means on my phone. In Antigua, I was using a basic phone. Dumbphone is what they're called. It's good having a smart phone. This is Mum's old phone. An ait is a small island in a river. *Dalton, what is an ait?*

'Ha, haha …'

Pupils are looking at me. I put the phone away and keep reading. *Fog on the Essex marshes, fog on the Kentish heights. Fog creeping into the cabooses of collier-brigs; fog lying out on the yards, and hovering in the rigging of great ships; fog drooping on the gunwales of barges and small boats. Fog in the eyes and throats of ancient Greenwich pensioners, wheezing by the firesides of their wards …*

The class is finished. It is time for the mid-morning break. Will head down to the basement, as it tends to be quieter there. At the bottom of the stairs, I lean against the wall and continue reading.

'Oi, cunt!' Think that was Dunce's big brother, Darragh, the head of the gang. I look up from the book. It is Darragh. 'Yeah you, new cunt.' He's standing right in front of me. 'Don't deal at or near school.'

'What makes you think—'

'Shut it! Know you were.' He steps forward and presses his massive chest into my chest. *Don't touch me.* 'You're new here 'n it's your first offence, so I'm being nice.' He blows air from his nose into my face. *Gross!* 'This is your one 'n only warning.'

He strides off and joins some other gang members in the corridor. Ah, this is so unfair, it should be a free market economy. Arsehole. Will just deal to Serena and her friends for now.

*

17:33 – I'm on the bus going to Serena's house. Went home after school and picked up some skunk. Mum's gone to the hospital again. Aunt Fatso still hasn't died. At least Mum is not making me go there anymore. Now she's in a coma, Mum doesn't think there's any point. Hasn't said so. Know that's why though. This is my stop. I get off, walk to the house, and ring the doorbell. Serena opens the door, throws her arms around my neck and kisses me on the mouth. She is wearing a skimpy pink T-shirt and white shorts that come halfway down her thighs. Dalilah, my girlfriend in Antigua, had similar shorts.

'Was playing netball, that's why I'm dressed like this.'

Her mother comes downstairs and says, 'Hi Horatio, good to see you. How're you getting on at your new school?'

'Don't like it.'

'Oh, what a pity. Would you like a Pepsi?'

'Yes please.'

We go through to the kitchen. It's big and full of top-end

utensils. Bet no kid at my school has a kitchen like this. We don't that's for sure. Half the size our kitchen and doesn't have any of these utensils. Serena's mother passes me a can of Pepsi. I say, 'Thank you.'

I open the can and have a gulp. They are talking in a corner of the room. Hear Serena's mother say, 'I don't want you in your room.'

'Whatever!'

Serena stomps over to me. Her mother says, 'See you two in a bit,' and walks out of the room.

Serena leans into me and whispers, 'Bring the gear?'

'Of course.'

I pass her a transparent seal bag containing four grammes of skunk. Weighed them on the kitchen scales at home. Serena passes me two twenty-pound notes.

'Two are for me, two are for a friend from school.' She tilts into me. 'Let's smoke some.'

'Okay. Got a bit on me; we'll smoke that.'

'Awesome.' Serena goes into the living room, stuffs the skunk in a cupboard, and hauls from the same cupboard a bong and some eye whitener drops. Back in the kitchen, she takes a small bottle of still mineral water from the fridge and puts it in a gym bag along with the bong. At the bottom of the stairs, she shouts, 'MUM!'

'Yes, sweety.'

'It's nice outside, we're going to the park for some fresh air.'

'Fine. Don't be too long though and answer your phone if I ring. Have *fun*. Oh, and put on some more clothes—'

Serena slams the front door shut. It's warm and sunny. About the only decent weather there's been since I returned from Antigua. Serena wraps her arm over my elbow.

'Lovely evening. London is so nice when it's sunny. Singapore is rank, well the weather is. Always humid. Feel gross, sweaty the whole time. Don't know how my father can live out there. Guess he's in the office most of the time. They'll have aircon.'

'Antigua can get quite clammy.'

'Singapore is super sweaty. And strict. Weed is bigtime illegal. For bringing it into the country, this Indian dude got executed. Over there, having this bong in my bag would be the same as having a bazooka.'

'Haha.'

'What's so funny?'

'You.'

'So I'm a comedian now?' She tugs on my arm. 'Never even smoked with you before. This'll be our first time.' We enter a park. 'Only started doing it when you were away. You?'

'Same. Smoked for the first time in Antigua. Loads of people smoke out there. It's decriminalised and you can have up to a certain amount on you. Police can't do anything.'

'Awesome.'

We pass a skateboard ramp. The skaters are staring at us. One wolf whistles. Another is staring so much he falls off his skateboard. Behind the skateboard ramp is this gated conservation area with a small pond with bushes on either side. Serena crouches down and goes into the bushes. I follow her. There is a small space in here enclosed on all sides. While pouring water into the bong, Serena says, 'Always smoke here if I'm with friends. Never on my own though, as could be dangerous cos no one can see you here.' I take the gramme of skunk I brought with me from my pocket, break some crumbs off and put them in the bong's bowl. Never smoked a bong before. Not going to tell Serena that though. 'Enough. Are you trying to blow my head off? Ladies first.' She lights the bong, the water makes a gargling noise, and a massive cloud of smoke is expelled from her mouth. She lights it again … 'Pokey this weed!'

It's my turn. I suck hard on the mouthpiece, remove my mouth, and breathe out. The smoke is ticklish, not like from a joint – 'Ahem, ahem …'

'Amateur.'

'It's ticklish.'

'There's more in there. Light it.' We both have a second bong. Serena pours the dirty water from the bong onto the ground. 'Stoned.' She blows on the bowl, wraps a tissue over it, puts the bong in her gym bag, then throws her arms around my neck, kisses me on the mouth and rubs herself against me. I am getting an erection. 'Turning you on this. I must be hot.' Can hear someone by the pond. We creep out of the bushes. There is a dumpy woman wearing green clothes. A park warden. She is looking at us. We hurry off. Serena giggles. 'Do you think she thought we were getting it on, or smoking weed?'

'Both most likely.'

'Looked pissed off. Probably jealous. We're smoking, she's working, and no skaters are wolf-whistling at her.'

When we arrive at the house, Serena gets two packets of Monster Munch from the kitchen. Excellent, I have the munchies. She collapses on the sofa in the living room and switches on the PlayStation 5. She has two games, *NBA 2K23* and *Spider-Man*. Serena says, 'The NBA game is my friend's boyfriend's. She left it here the other day. Kind of sucks. Want to play?'

We play. She's not wrong. By PlayStation 5 standards, this is pretty poor. Her mother comes in, and says, 'What did you two do in the park?'

Serena says, 'Walked around the pond.'

I say, 'Watched kids skateboarding on the ramp.'

'I'll bring you some hors d'oeuvres.'

She leaves the room. Serena kisses me on the cheek, and says, 'Couldn't bring myself to tell Mum we smoked bongs and you got a hard-on.'

Her mother comes in with a plate of food, and says, 'Olives, crostini with goat's cheese, and stuffed mushrooms.'

Serena takes the plate off her, and says, 'Thanks. *Bye*.' Her mother sighs and walks off. 'Close the door!'

'No, I'm going to leave it open.'

'Whatever.' The olives and crostini are tasty. The mushrooms are pretty rank though. Serena puts a mushroom in her mouth, screws up her face, spits the mushroom into a tissue and throws it in the bin. 'Squelchy. Gross. What was Mum thinking buying those? Let's play *Spider-Man*.'

We play for an hour. Then I leave. Will see Serena again soon. It is quarter to eight and still light. In Antigua it'd be dark by now. Sunset and sunrise are at a similar time all year round. Only varies by an hour or so, unlike here. Gets dark quickly over there too. It's because Antigua is not far north of the equator. My bus has just left. While I'm waiting for another bus, Mum phones and asks where I am. I tell her I'm quite hungry. She says she'll make something light for us. Serena and her mother have guests coming at eight for dinner. That's why I didn't have a full meal. Mum better not be making salad. Here comes the bus. Wasn't too long a wait. I board it and find a seat near the back on the lower deck. Need to get some earphones, so don't have to listen to idiots talking. I should have brought *Bleak House* with me. Wouldn't have read much though, it's not far.

Arrived. I get off the bus. It's pretty crowded. I weave through the people, turn the corner, and keep walking. On the other side of the street can see two men approaching from the opposite direction. One of them is short and stocky, the other tall and skinny. As they get closer, I notice the skinny man has a really long nose. Rat. What the hell's he doing here? He's seen me.

'OI!' There are two of them, so I'm going to run. I sprint along the pavement. They've crossed the road and are pursuing me. 'Horatio, know you did it. You murdering scum!'

I race along the street, swerve around the corner into my street and keep running, pulling the housekey from my pocket as I go. They have disappeared. I unlock the front door and go inside. Mum comes out of the kitchen.

'You're out of breath, what have you been doing?'

'Running.'

'Why?'

'Because I felt like it.'

'Food's ready, wash your hands.'

I rinse my hands in the kitchen sink. Why the hell was Rat there? Seems highly unlikely it was a coincidence. He must've suspected I was back living here. And now he knows I am, which is not good. Two pieces of bread-crumbed chicken and lettuce. Could be worse, a lot worse. Mum says, 'Ketchup or chilli sauce?'

'Both.'

'Please.'

'Please.'

We sit down and eat. Mum lowers her fork to her plate, and says, 'Did you have fun at Serena's?'

'Yeah, it was good.'

'Got back from the hospital an hour ago. A-hh, just want the nightmare to end.' I sever off a piece of chicken and put it in my mouth. Mum murmurs, 'Will be a relief when it's over.' She scrunches her eyes shut then opens them. 'Been trying to keep my mind occupied, so don't think about it all the time. This morning I cleaned the house top to bottom. Was going to go to Tanice's flat to sort out some stuff. But can't bring myself to go round there right now—' *SMASH!* That was in the living room. We race into the living room. The window has been smashed and there is a brick on the floor. *Rat!* 'Oh my God!' Mum covers her mouth with her palm. She removes it, runs into the hallway, opens the front door and goes outside. I follow her. The street is empty. We go back inside. She is looking at me. 'Who would do such a thing?'

I shrug my shoulders. Mum screams, 'AHHH! Could do without this.' She collapses to a sitting position on the floor and holds her head in her hands. Want to kill Rat, slowly. He deserves pain, and lots of it. Mum stays on the floor for several minutes before sighing and standing up. 'Wanton destruction. It was probably kids. Best report it to the police, not that they'll do anything.' She curls her fingers. 'I'll phone them. You get a dustpan and brush, bin liners and tape from the kitchen. We'll just have to cover it for now.'

THREE

TWO DAYS LATER – In the second class of the day, English. *Jane Eyre* is lying open on my desk. I am thinking about Rat. With any luck that brick was the end of it. Regardless, thinking isn't going to help. Rat is too insignificant to spend time thinking about anyway. Underneath the desk, I'm holding *Bleak House.* Good book this; no wonder my father owned a copy. Only thing is there are a lot of old, outdated words I have to look up. Antiquated is the term that would be used to describe them. At a desk two rows to my left, Dunce is smirking at me. He has no reason to smirk. I look at him and mouth *anti-quat-ed.* At the desk in front of him, Tricia has rotated around. She blows a kiss at me. Dunce isn't smirking now; he is snarling.

'Horatio!' That was the teacher. 'It's your turn to read.'

Where are we? The Bangladeshi girl leans across the aisle and points at the place on the page. I stand up and read – 'In five minutes more the cloud of bewilderment dissolved: I knew quite well that I was in my own bed, and that the red glare was the nursery fire. It was night: a candle burnt on the table; Bessie stood at the bed-foot with a basin in her hand, and a gentleman sat in a chair near my pillow, leaning over me ...'

The teacher is dividing the class into groups of five. She puts me in a group with three girls. Dumbasses all of them. Well, the Bangladeshi is pretty good at maths and science I suppose, compared to the others anyway. For the fifth member of our group, the teacher selects Dunce. Oh no, the moron supremo. After putting the rest of the class into groups, she says, 'We are going to discuss themes in *Jane Eyre*. By theme, we mean an idea that recurs in the novel … Each group will choose a theme. You will discuss it with your group and then together with the class. Got it?' There are murmured yeses and groans. *Will go with irony. Have loads of examples.* 'Get together in your groups.'

Bollocks, it involves moving. My group have gathered at one of the girl's desks. I carry my chair over to her desk. Dunce drags his chair over and dumps himself on it. He looks a bit like a bull terrier – stocky, ugly, small pointy ears. His smudge nose sort of ruins the look though. The teacher gives each group an A3 piece of paper, and says, 'Write *Jane Eyre* at the top, your theme underneath, and the reasons for choosing it with examples.'

Dunce takes a red pen off the girl's desk. It's the same colour as the gang's graffiti. He is writing on the A3 paper. What a surprise, he knows how to write. Big letters these. JANE AIR.

'HA, HAHA, HAHAHA!'

'What you laughin' for, bruv?'

'HAHAHA, HAHAHA …'

'Stop laughin'!'

One of the girls is giggling. I am bent forward laughing non-stop – 'HAHAHA!' Dunce shoves me in my shoulder. My eyes are watering. 'HAHAHA.'

He shoves me again and spits, 'Don't be disrespectin' me. Will fuck you up!'

'HAHAHA …'

The teacher comes over and says, 'Care to share what's so funny?'

'Nothin',' says Dunce. 'He's lost it.'

I stand up, wipe my eyes with my sleeve, and say loudly so the whole class can hear, 'Dalton, haha, spelt Eyre like the air you breathe. A-I-R.'

Dunce leaps off his chair and shouts, 'Will stab you up!'

'HAHA ...'

Not many pupils are laughing, which is strange, as this is hilarious. Dunce punches me in the arm. I move to the other side of the desk and continue laughing. Dunce picks up the chair he was sitting on. The teacher screeches, 'Dalton, put it down!' He hurls it at me, I tilt to the side, the chair smashes on the floor. The Bangladeshi girl is shrieking, pupils are scampering to the other end of the classroom, others out of the classroom. The teacher is holding onto Dunce's arm and screeching, 'Stop it!'

'Stab you!'

'Ha, haha ...'

Dunce pulls free from the teacher's grip and charges around the desk. The teacher grabs him by the waist. He wrests her off and she falls to the floor. He is right in front of me, snarling, 'Stab you up!' I raise my hands to my chin. Two male teachers bundle into the room and sprint over to Dunce. He tells them to, 'Fuck off!' then lunges at me with his right hand. I slip my head to the side. The two teachers grab a hold of his arms and drag him away. 'Stab you!' He spits a mouthful of phlegm at me. It lands on the floor. *Disgusting.* He is squirming to break free. My teacher grabs Dunce's ankles and lifts them up. He is carried out of the classroom. 'WAHHH!'

Can still hear him screaming in the corridor. Jane Air – that is the funniest thing ever. Everyone is looking at me. Some of them are shaking their heads. A girl says, 'Will pay bigtime for disrespecting him. You get me?'

A boy says, 'You'll be watching your back forever.'

Tricia's mouth is hanging open. Can see chewing gum in it. She says, 'Must have a death wish. And I thought you were clever.'

I am. She closes her mouth and chews. By the time the teacher returns, the class is virtually over. Dunce isn't in the next class. The moron will have been sent home for going mental. Ten minutes before the class ends, a teacher comes in and says the headmaster wants to talk to me. I go to his office. He is sitting behind his desk. He takes off his glasses and says, 'Sit.' I sit on a chair on the other side of the desk. 'I have been informed of the disturbance in class. Dalton's been sent home for violent disorder. My understanding is it was you who set him off. You were laughing at him. Why?'

'He spelt the Eyre in Jane Eyre, A-I-R.'

'*He.* A-hem, something stuck in my throat.' He looks up at the ceiling, then at me. 'Now I appreciate it was a quite extraordinary thing for Dalton to do. But try and be more supportive of your classmates in future. Dalton needs encouragement, not mocking. Is that understood?' I nod. 'Would strongly recommend not antagonising that boy when he returns from suspension. He is extremely volatile, as you are now aware. That'll be all.'

During the mid-morning break, members of the Daggerz gang come over to me and make stabbing gestures in the air. They tell me *Darragh is pissed off bigtime* and my life won't be worth living. He's already annoyed with me for dealing near school. In the next class, French, I think about the situation. What's the worst that could happen? Get punched or kicked a few times. I will give it back to them if it happens. Anyway, hopefully Dunce won't be returning anytime soon. This school is slack and has almost no discipline. The headmaster surely though has to punish pupils severely for threatening to stab people. My guess is Dunce will be gone at least a week. When he returns, he won't want more trouble. If he does try to stab me, he'll be suspended or expelled. Dunce is an idiot though, so anything is possible.

At lunchtime I get more warnings from members of the Daggerz gang and from other pupils. But no one tries to do anything to me. I'm now in the last class of the week, geography. The class is nearly over when my phone beeps. It is a text.

Today, Now

Come straight home from school Pls. Mum XX

Always come straight home from school, well pretty much anyway. When the class ends, I make my way along the corridors. Am a couple of metres from the hallway when I hear behind me, 'Cunt!' *Darragh.* I turn around. 'Getting on my tits you are, new cunt.' Could run off, same as with Rat. However, gang members are blocking the corridor ahead of me. Darragh is striding this way. He steps into my personal space, pushes his massive chest into me and presses me against the wall. *Go away!* 'My little bruver has learning difficulties. 'N he's not getting the support he needs to overcome them. It's not funny. 'N no cunt better think it is. Alright?' He steps back. 'This matter will be dealt with when Dalton's back. Jog on!'

I walk off. The gang members are laughing at me. I clench my fists. How dare they? I go outside. This is so unfair. It's Dunce's problem, not his big brother's. Can't even deal with his own problems. He is a loser and a coward. What are they planning?

*

I don't run into Rat on the way home. Mum and my sister are in the kitchen. My sister is visiting from college again. Mum is bent forward in her chair with her face in her hands. My sister is standing beside the chair with one hand resting on Mum's shoulder.

'A-hhh.' Mum lifts her head. 'Horatio.'

'Yeah.'

They are both staring at me. Mum's eyes are puffy and tears are trickling down my sister's cheeks. Mum says, 'There's no easy way to say this. Earlier this afternoon, a-hh, Tanice, passed away.'

That was easy. My sister says, 'Always thought she'd be here forever, or at least until I was pretty old. That she'd be there when I got married and had children. Waah ...!'

My sister is crying non-stop. No more visits to the hospital; no more Aunt Fatso telling me what to do. Mum grabs my wrist and pulls me to her. My sister collapses onto a chair, pushes her face into Mum's shoulder and continues crying. Mum says, 'Sit,' *sniff*, 'down.'

When she releases her grip on my wrist, I sit down. My sister stops crying and looks at me with wet eyes.

'At least she's not suffering anymore and is in heaven.'

Malteser Heaven. More likely scenario is she was too bossy during her life and was denied entry. She's in hell. A hell similar to what Tantalus faced in Greek mythology. Aunt Fatso's in a pool of Coca-Cola up to her chin and hovering above her are Maltesers. Every time she tries to grab them, they hover up out of reach. Bit like drones they are. And every time she tries to take a drink, the Coca-Cola dries up. This goes on and on for eternity. I put my forearm over my mouth to stop myself laughing. Will wait here for five minutes, otherwise they'll be angry with me for leaving. Between sobs my sister says how much she loved Aunt Fatso. She starts wailing again ... Right, that's five minutes. I go upstairs to my room. Haven't been in there long when there is a knock on the door.

'Horatio.' *Mum.* 'Can I come in?'

'Yeah.'

She comes in – 'How're you feeling?'

'Okay, I guess.'

'Knew it was coming and it's, ah, not as if Tanice had any hope of recovery. Still a big shock somehow though that's she's gone. A-hh, at least she's not suffering anymore.' *Sniff.* 'We're popping out for a walk. Do you want to come with us?'

'I'm good.'

'Will you be alright here.' *Sniff.* 'We won't be long.'

'Yeah.'

'See you in a bit.'

She closes the door. I pick up my father's black snakeskin tie. The perfect event is coming up to showcase this tie. My phone is ringing. It's Serena.

'Hi.'

'Hey gorgeous, what's up?'

'Not a lot.'

'Had a netball match against another school this afternoon. We won. Since I got home been in my room using *TikTok*. School was *so* boring as usual. How was your day?'

'Laughed at this idiot in my class. He threatened to stab me and got suspended.'

'Oh my God! What a loser.'

'Yeah.'

'Laugh at girls at my school all the time. It's no big deal.' *But those girls' big brother isn't Darragh.* 'Don't worry he won't stab you. Don't think so anyway. The only kid I've ever known who stabbed someone is you. That idiot at our old school in art class.'

'He deserved it.'

'Sure did. Have you told your mum yet it was the rat dude who threw the brick through your window?'

'No.'

'You have to, he could be dangerous. Your family need to know there's a psycho who has it in for you.' *I told Serena about it yesterday.* 'Are you listening?'

'Yeah.'

'Tell your mum what's going on with him. She needs to know … What're you up to?'

'I'm looking at my new tie.'

'Tie, *okay*. What's this tie look like?'

'Black.'

'Cheery. You're not planning to become a goth, are you? If you are, we're so done. Goths suck.'

'It's stylish this tie. Used to belong to my father. Mum gave me some of his stuff the other day. She'd kept it for me. It's made of black snakeskin. Python, I think.'

'This tie is getting more interesting. Show me.' I turn on *FaceTime* and hold the tie up to the camera. 'Sleek. Must've been expensive. When are you going to wear it?'

'At the funeral.'

'Funeral?'

'My aunt's.'

'She died!'

'Yeah, today.'

'Your aunt died and you're telling me about your tie.'

*

Three days later – School is over for the day. Dunce is still suspended. With any luck, he won't be returning anytime soon. As I walk home from the bus stop, I keep half an eye out for Rat. Childish of him breaking that window. The window has now been fixed. Hopefully seen the last of Rat. He is really pissed off with me though, and I suspect he's not done yet. Mum's father flew in from Antigua earlier this afternoon, but fortunately his bossy wife didn't come. He might already be at the house. It's going to be busy; my sister is still staying.

Can hear Mum talking on the telephone upstairs. Don't think her father or my sister are here. I get a glass of orange juice from the fridge and go to the living room. The furniture is still as the tenants had it. Want to return it to the way it should be, the way it used to be, the way it was when I killed Fool's Gold. Mum is not going to allow it though. I switch on the television and flick through the channels. There isn't much on, so I watch the news. Mum barges into the living room.

'Turn the TV off, your grandfather's here.'

I join her in the hallway. The front door opens revealing Mum's father and my sister. She must have picked him up from the tube station, or the airport. Mum lurches forward and throws her arms around her father's neck. My sister is hugging his waist. They release their grip. He slaps me on the shoulder, and says, 'Hello grandson.'

'Hi.'

Mum says, 'Horatio, take your grandfather's suitcase up to his room.' I lug his wheeled suitcase upstairs to my sister's room. She is sleeping in Mum's room. I look over the banister. They are hugging him again. I go into my room and sit at my desk. About to start my maths homework when the door swings open. It's Mum. She closes the door and puts her fists on her hips. 'What're you doing?'

'My homework.'

'Downstairs, now!' *Ahh!* I go downstairs. Mum walks behind me with her palm pushed into my lower back. 'Offer him a drink.'

We go into the kitchen. Mum's father and my sister are in here. I say, 'Would you like a drink?'

'Yes,' he says. 'Thank you. A beer if you have any.'

'We do,' says Mum.

I get a bottle of beer from the fridge, open it, and give it to him. We all sit at the kitchen table. They are discussing Aunt Fatso. Mum's father places his hand on Mum's shoulder, and says, 'It's incredibly hard on you having to organise the funeral.'

'Yeah. Shaneeka's a big help though.'

'Good girl.' He places his other hand on my sister's shoulder. 'You've always been a great help to your mother.'

'Do what I can.' My sister turns to face him. 'I haven't seen you in ages. Was hoping it would be a happy time when we saw each other.'

'You and me both. But it can't be helped, unfortunately.'

They are discussing the funeral arrangements. Mum's father says, 'I would like to choose a bouquet for her.'

'Of course,' says Mum. 'We've got an appointment at the funeral parlour tomorrow at three. We'll see what they've got.' She shakes her head and murmurs, 'Same place that did Brandon's funeral.' *Fool's Gold.* 'Can't believe I'm being faced with another funeral already.'

My sister gets off her chair and hugs Mum. Her father bows his head and mutters, 'Terrible, it really is.'

No one says anything, they just sit there. This is boring, I want to go up to my room. Mum's father says he could do with a walk after being *cooped up on the plane for so long.*

My sister says, 'I'll come with you; we'll go to the park.'

'Good idea,' says Mum. 'I'll start preparing dinner.'

Mum's father says, 'Give me a minute to get ready.'

He leaves the room. Mum says, 'Horatio, while I start on dinner, you can put your laundry on and lay the table.'

I go into the hallway. My sister is there. I ask her, 'What's happening with Tanice's will? Are we getting anything?'

She tugs on my wrist and says through the side of her mouth, 'Don't mention the will again. Got it?'

I go upstairs, haul the dirty laundry from the basket in my bedroom, go down to the kitchen, shove it in the washing machine along with a capsule, pour softener in the dispenser drawer, and select a forty-degree wash. Could almost be back working in the launderette in Antigua. There it was the manager bossing me about, here it is Mum. That launderette was a bloody nightmare; the worst way imaginable to spend my Saturdays. However, school was better over there.

Done two-thirds of my maths homework when I hear the front door close. Mum will be up in a minute ordering me downstairs. Might as well go down now. In the kitchen, my sister says, 'We had a nice walk. Was good catching up.'

'Certainly was, darling. A lovely evening it is too.'

Mum says, 'You brought the Antiguan weather with you.'

'Yes, seems so.' Mum's father swipes his palm across his cheek.

'Rakesha, when we returned from the park there was a man hanging around outside on the street. He was looking suspicious. Cleared off sharpish when he saw us. I thought I should let you know.'

Rat! Mum looks up at the ceiling and murmurs something. She looks at her father, and says, 'Been a few strange goings on here of late.'

She tells him about the brick being thrown through the living room window. My sister taps my arm, and whispers, 'Come upstairs.'

I follow her upstairs. In the passageway, she says breathlessly, 'Think it was Brandon's friend, Rollie. Couldn't tell for sure because he was wearing a hooded top. But he was tall, skinny, and I got a glimpse of his nose. It was long, exceedingly long.' *Rat alright.* 'Probably wouldn't even have occurred to me it was him, if it wasn't for the tenants saying they'd seen a man loitering who fitted Rollie's description.' She sucks on her lower lip. 'Why would he be here?' I shrug my shoulders. 'Doesn't make any sense.' She rubs the back of her head. 'Don't want to worry Mum, she has enough on her plate as it is. And if she thinks it's him, will bring back memories of Brandon and the terrible time we had when he …' She screws her eyes shut. 'Maybe it wasn't him, maybe it was someone else, waiting to buy drugs or something.' She opens her eyes. 'Why would he be hanging around here?'

FOUR

THE FOLLOWING SATURDAY – Aunt Fatso's funeral is this morning. It's in Newton, which is half an hour's drive from here. I found out online my father was head of the Burials and Cemeteries department at Newton Council. We are going to the funeral in my dead aunt's car. It belongs to Mum now. Guess she'll inherit her flat too. I asked Mum about the will. She said she didn't want to discuss it, and I was not to mention it.

Am in the bathroom, looking at my reflection in the mirror above the sink. I am wearing the dark grey suit and the black snakeskin tie my father left me. Will definitely be the most stylish person there. There aren't going to be many people there. She wasn't popular. I leave the bathroom. Mum is in the passageway, wearing the same outfit she wore for Fool's Gold's funeral.

'You look so smart and grown up. The suit fits you almost perfectly.' The jacket is no more than a centimetre too long. She runs her fingertips down my left arm. 'Remember your father wearing that suit.'

'At Newton Council?'

'Yes!' She retracts her head. 'Don't remember telling you that.'

'I found some stuff online when I was in Antigua.'

'Oh!'

'There were some articles about his work. He was head of the Burials and Cemeteries department at Newton Council, which means he would have been to the place where the funeral is being held today.'

'Most likely, yeah.' Mum pats my arm. 'Go downstairs and chat with the others. And I needn't remind you to be on your best behaviour today.'

My sister and Mum's father are in the kitchen. No one seems to go in the living room much these days, other than me. My sister is wearing the same outfit she wore for Fool's Gold's funeral – a black, tight-fitting trouser suit. While they chat, I pour myself a glass of water. Mum's father presses the balls of his palms to his temples, and says, 'Awful I never got to see my daughter again. Was planning to come, but then Tanice suddenly went downhill. I could've flown straight over. Couldn't face seeing my daughter like that though.' He sighs. 'I feel so guilty.'

'Don't feel guilty, Granddad.' My sister hugs his arm with both of hers. 'Tanice would totally understand. I know she would.'

He covers his face with his hands. Mum comes into the kitchen, walks up to me, grips my right hand, raises it, and puts it on her father's shoulder.

*

The chapel, funeral hall and crematorium are in the middle of the cemetery we are walking through. This is the largest cemetery I've ever been in. Larger than the cemetery where Fool's Gold was buried, and that was pretty big. On either side of the path are graves. On the corners of some of them are white cherubs. A few years ago, I visited the National Gallery with my class. Some of the Renaissance paintings had cherubs in them. They could be described as elegant. This lot look like out of shape kids who have eaten way too much fast food. My father wouldn't have appreciated these cherubs, that's for sure. He had good taste in clothes; the same would've gone for cherubs. Mum stops on the steps outside the chapel.

'Are you ready?'

Her father nods, and my sister says, 'Yes Mum.'

'Horatio?'

'Yeah.'

'You know what you have to do.'

I am carrying the casket with Mum's father and two others. Good thing she lost a load of weight, or we'd have to drag her casket down the aisle like a sledge. We go inside. No one is here. The chapel door opens. So, someone's come. It's the chaplain. He doesn't count, as this is compulsory for him.

Twenty-five minutes later – I am standing next to the casket. Me and my aunt's ex-work colleague are carrying the rear. Mum's father is carrying the front with a second cousin. Think he is a second cousin. I've met him before a few times. Classical music is playing. We pick up the casket and carry it into the chapel. Doesn't weigh much at all. Remarkable what disease and not gorging on chocolate for a few months did for her weight. We walk slowly along the aisle. Other than my family, there are only seven people here, guests that is. There are also five choristers. A chorister is a term for a member of a choir. Came across that word in an order of service at a church in Antigua. Could count on one hand the number of pupils at my school who would know what a chorister is. We lower the casket and go to our seats. I am sitting at the end of the front pew next to my sister.

The service is dragging on. I check the time on my Swatch. Twenty-seven minutes it's been going on for. When the casket was carried in at the start of Fool's Gold's funeral, the music was supposed to be *Never Say Goodbye* by Bon Jovi. However, I sneaked into the room where the music system was and changed it. Because everyone thought he had died from auto erotic asphyxiation gone wrong, I chose the theme tune for *Top Gun*. *Take My Breath Away*. Fool's Gold's father went berserk, as did Rat. It was hilarious. Much funnier even than Dunce spelling the Eyre in *Jane Eyre*, A-I-R. Rat accused me of changing the music.

Didn't accuse me of killing Fool's Gold though. But he was suspicious; he was questioning me before the funeral.

Think he decided I'd killed him for sure after the funeral, at the burial in the cemetery. I phoned the police and told them Rat was trying to abuse children. I'd put erotic asphyxiation materials, paraphernalia, in his bag. The police searched Rat and took him away. Screaming, he was – *Devil Cunt.* I bite the sleeve of my suit jacket to stop myself laughing … *Take my breath away.* I clamp down with my teeth and try to think of something serious … Maths, physics, equations. I repeat the words in my mind. *Maths, physics, equations. Maths, physics, equations* … Mum and my sister are glaring at me. I release my teeth and lower my arm.

Ah, another hymn. Nearly as bad as church in Antigua this. Over there they had a hymn every two minutes. It's *Amazing Grace.*

'Amazing grace how sweet the sound
That saved a wretch like me
I once was lost, but now I'm found
Was blind but now …'

I mouth the words. The choristers sing them loudly. It would be dead in here without them. Mum goes to the front of the chapel to do a reading.

'*She is Gone* by David Harkins.' She inflates and deflates her cheeks. 'You can shed tears that she is gone, a-hh, or you can smile because she has lived.' *I'm doing neither.* 'You can close your eyes and pray, a-hh, that she will come back.' *She better not.* 'Or you can open your eyes, a-hh, a-hh …' *Pull it together Mum, you're being embarrassing.* 'And see all she has left.' *Flat, money, car.* 'Your heart can be empty because you can't see her …'

This is the best tie ever. Will wear it for every single funeral I ever go to. Wish I'd had it for Fool's Gold's. The chaplain asks everyone to kneel and reflect on their time with Tanice. When I close my eyes, I see her cramming handfuls of Maltesers into her gob … Finally, it's the last hymn. *Morning Has Broken.*

'Morning has broken like the first morning
Blackbird has spoken like the first bird
Praise for the singing, praise for the morning
Praise for them springing fresh from the world ...'

My family and the seven other people who have come go through to the funeral hall for tea. Post-funeral refreshments are called a repast. Saw the term on the funeral order of service. *Dunce, what's a repast ...? Some-ink to do with the past, innit?* There is a chocolate cake Aunt Fatso would have devoured. Should really have Maltesers embedded in it. I help myself to a large slice. It has layers of cream and tastes good. My sister comes over to me.

'You could have offered cake to other people.'

Could have, yeah. My second cousin or whoever he is chats with me. He wants to know all about my time in Antigua. Says he hasn't been there since he was a kid. After the repast, the guests leave. Me, my sister, Mum and her father go through to the crematorium for the cremation. There is an observation room with a massive flat screen television on the wall. I sit on a chair, they sit on a cream-coloured leather sofa. A raging furnace appears on the screen. Here she goes. The casket is engulfed in flames. They all start crying, and they don't stop. If she was still fat, molten blubber would be being spat all over the screen. They're crying turns to whimpering and sobbing. Aunt Fatso better have left me something.

*

It's Monday morning, and I'm in the second class of the day, geography. Dunce is back. He is sitting at a desk three rows in front. Was smirking at me non-stop all through history. Dunce twists around in his seat and smirks at me again. Why is he looking so pleased with himself? What is he planning? Tricia is looking at me. Her mouth is held in a horizontal line and she is shaking her head. I nibble on a fingernail. Wouldn't be concerned if it was just that idiot. The problem is his big brother. The teacher is explaining how a coastal landscape is a section of coastline that has a range of coastal features. I am tapping the base of my pen on the desk.

'Hehe, hehe …'

That's Dunce. Why's he laughing? The teacher says, 'Dalton, something funny?'

'Nah!'

'We'll continue then. A high energy coastal environment is dominated by developing features of erosion …'

The class is over and pupils are rushing out of the classroom. There goes Dunce. Good, the moron is getting on my nerves. Wish he was still suspended, or even better expelled. As Tricia leaves the classroom, she looks at me and scrunches up her nose. I will go down to the basement. With any luck won't be too many pupils there and it'll be quiet enough to read *Bleak House*. Still got a lot to get through. It's a very long book, over a thousand pages.

In the basement, I lean against the wall near the stairs, eat a Snickers and read. Can hear pupils stomping down the stairs. Lots of them. I look up from *Bleak House*. Oh no, it's Darragh. Dunce is following behind him with other members of the gang, boys and girls. Best get out of here. I hurry off along the corridor. The gang are marching this way. Will scoot through the exit by the changing rooms at the end of the corridor. Up ahead, I see a grotesquely fat sixth former with his arms folded blocking the exit. *Damn!* The gang are still marching this way. I weave between two girls and approach the fat sixth former.

'Want to get past.'

'Nah, not happening.'

Ah, the gang are here. They form two lines behind Darragh across the width of the corridor. Darragh tilts his chin up and pushes his massive chest out.

'Shut up 'n listen!' Everyone immediately stops talking, except the two girls I just weaved between. A blonde and a brown girl with a bindi dot. Darragh thrusts a finger at them. 'Shut it!'

The girl with the bindi says, 'Ah, me?'

'Yeah you, the one with the red dot in the middle of your fucking head.' The gang laugh. 'Been doing a lot of cosying up with little Miss Blondie, in't yah, Minge-ita.' The gang laugh louder. The bindi girl's mouth is hanging open. He has a quicker wit than his little brother. There is silence. 'During the breaks, morning 'n afternoon, if you lot haven't got business with us in the boys changing room, stay the fuck away from this end of the corridor. Jog on!' The gang parts in the middle and the pupils scuttle between them. I go in the same direction. 'Not you, cunt.'

The gang closes ranks, blocking me in. *Ah!* Dunce smirks and says, 'To the bogs!'

Gang members grab me by the arms and legs and pick me up. *No!* My mini rucksack is hanging from my shoulder. *Bleak House* drops from my hand. They haul me along the corridor.

'Get off me!' I try to wrest my arms and legs free, but they are being held firmly. 'You can't do this to me! It's assault.'

They carry me along the length of the corridor to the boys' toilets. My ankles are released and my feet slam on the floor. What do they want from me? I would run off if my arms weren't still being held. Darragh bellows, 'Finish up 'n get the fuck aht!'

Boys scurry from the cubicles and urinals. *What's going on?* Everyone else has gone. It's just me and the gang. A sixth former is leaning against the door. I'm trapped. Darragh and his smirking little brother are standing in front of me.

'All I did was laugh—'

'Zip it!' Darragh presses his thick right index finger into my chin. *Ah!* 'If you're planning to rat us aht to the teachers, be aware they'll find aht about this.' He clicks his fingers. A girl passes him a phone. It's the same girl who was with the boy I dealt to in the alleyway by the bus stop. Darragh is holding the screen towards me. It is a video of me passing that boy the skunk and taking his money. Can clearly see the drugs, money, and my face. This is so unfair. 'Autistic he is. Teachers will be told you'd been pushing him hard to buy drugs. They'll love that.'

'What do you want from me?' Darragh slaps my head. *Ow!* 'Let go of me.'

'Shut your trap 'n take your punishment like a man. Bruver.' He places his hands on Dunce's shoulders. 'I'm off. Do it proper. 'N don't drown the cunt.'

Drown! What're they going to do, waterboard me? 'Let me go!' Darragh leaves. 'NOW!' The girl who took the video shoves a filthy sock in my mouth. 'B-B-B ...'

Dunce says, 'Load 'er up.'

Load what up? The fat sixth former who was blocking the exit to the corridor waddles into a cubicle and shuts the door. There is a loud *splash*! That came from the cubicle. He is taking a dump. I've got to get out of here. I writhe my left arm free. But it is grabbed again and I am punched in the stomach. *Ow!* I bend forward. *Splash ...!* That is one disgusting smell. *Eeew!* And I can only breathe through my nose because of the filthy sock in my mouth. Dunce and the other gang members put their mouths and noses beneath their tops. A girl says, 'Stinks!'

And a boy, 'You're an animal, Mustapha.'

'You're a wrong 'un,' screeches the only other girl in here, Tricia's older sister. 'Rank!'

Why isn't Tricia here? She likes me; she will help me. Tricia's sister pushes the boy leaning on the door out of the way, opens the door, and sticks her head out. I am punched in the stomach again; the air is driven from my lungs. The door to the cubicle bursts open, the fat sixth former waddles out and fastens his belt. *Help!* Dunce is standing in front of me with his nose and mouth under his top. I try and suck air through my mouth but can't with the sock stuffed in it. I inhale through my nose. Yuck, it's the worst smell ever. My blazer is pulled off. Tricia's sister unbuttons my shirt and says, 'Don't get the wrong idea.' I try to tell her through my stuffed mouth to get Tricia. All that comes out though is a muffled noise. She retches. 'Jesus Christ Mustapha, it stinks. You're never getting in my pants after that shit.'

There is roaring laughter. I have to escape. My shirt is pulled off. *Ahh!* Dunce says, 'Get 'im up; get 'im under.'

I am hoisted upside down and carried by my ankles into the cubicle where the fat sixth former did the shit. The sock is plucked from my mouth – 'HELP!' I am lifted higher. 'NO! NO! NO!' Not in the toilet. My head is hanging over the toilet bowl, which is crammed full of brown slop. 'BLRGH!' My hands are on the toilet seat, and I am pushing up with all my strength. 'HELP! HELP!'

'Don't be shy.' That was Tricia's sister. 'Get in there.'

'STOP!' My arms are pulled away. 'AHHH!' I descend head-first into the bowl. Shit mushes against the top of my head. I am hauled up. 'NO!' Down I go. The toilet is flushed. Water and shit are going into my nose and mouth. My feet smack on the floor. I pull my head out of the toilet. 'BLRGH!'

They are all laughing. Dunce the loudest – 'HEHEHE ...!'

Ah! I am alone in the cubicle with toilet water streaming from my hair. The laughs are fainter now. I crawl out of the cubicle and over to the basins. The gang are gone. I grip onto a basin's rim and haul myself up. In the mirror above the basin, I see my reflection. My hair is sopping and there are chunks of shit and bits of wet bog roll in it.

'RAHHH!'

I wash my mouth out with water then empty soap from the soap dispenser onto my palms, turn on the taps, shove my head in the basin, rub the soap into my hair, then run my knuckles across my scalp. I hear a boy say, 'Stinks in here, bruv.'

Another, 'Worst shit *ever*!'

Ow, the hot water is burning me. I turn off the hot tap then douse my head and face with cold water. Will torture and kill them all for this. I reel away from the basin, shout, 'DIE!' and throw a flurry of punches in the air. This is so unfair; how could this happen to me? I dry my hair under a hairdryer. My shirt, jacket and mini rucksack are on the floor. I dropped *Bleak House* in the corridor. I need it; it was my father's. Having pulled on my shirt and jacket, I grab the mini rucksack, exit the toilets, and race along the corridor. It isn't here. *No!* I enter the boys' changing rooms. No one is in here. I slump on a bench. French has already started. No way I'm going. Will torture them all to death for this, slowly, medieval style. This school sucks, it would never have happened at my other schools.

'RAHHH!'

French is nearly over, and I am still slumped on the bench in the changing rooms with my hands covering my face. I remove them and sniff the air. Can still smell that shit. I leap off the bench and pound my fists on the wall. Their remains will be impaled on the railings outside school, Vlad The Impaler-style. And left to rot.

I collapse onto the bench. There is noise in the corridor. It better not be the Daggerz. *No! No!* The changing room door bursts open and boys from the year below me pour in. They must have PE class. I squeeze through them into the corridor. The last class before lunchbreak is physics. No way I'm going, I can't face Dunce. Why's he even doing physics? He won't be taking individual sciences for his GCSEs because he's too thick. Will be doing combined sciences. It's irrelevant anyway, as by then he'll be a skeleton impaled on the railings outside school.

Will bunk off and go to the park. I leave via the basement exit and go up the steps to the street. Someone is waving at me from a ground floor window. It's the Dinka. What does she want? Am walking along the pavement when she strides up to me, and says, 'Didn't you see me waving? This is yours, right?' She is holding a book, my father's book, *Bleak House*. 'During the mid-morning break popped out to the shops. When I came back it was on the basement corridor's floor. It's yours, seen you reading it before.'

I take it off her and say, 'Thanks.'

'Where are you going?'

'To the park.'

'Bunking class?'

'Yes.'

'Unlike you. Everything alright, your eyes are red.'

In the park, I stare at the pond and imagine torturing them using a power drill and an electric saw. Not returning to school today, as can't face any of them, especially not Dunce, unless it's to kill him, slowly. My blazer smells of piss.

'*Fffff.*'

It's because it was on the floor of the toilets. Shirt is alright though because it was dropped on top of my blazer and didn't get piss on it. Got enough money in my mini rucksack to get McDonalds for lunch. While I'm there, will wipe my jacket in the toilets. They are so dead for this, especially Dunce. Their deaths will be far slower and more painful than the deaths of Fool's Gold and the drug dealer in Antigua. Don't want to return to that sorry excuse for a school ever again. I deserve the best school, not the worst. I get off the bench and kick a tree.

Four and a half hours later – 'RAH!'

I slap a lamppost. A woman with a pushchair coming from the opposite direction reels to the side. Before entering the house, I take some big breaths through my nose. When I go inside, Mum calls me from the kitchen. She is working from home today. I go into the kitchen.

'What?'

'Your school sent me an email. You were only there for the first two classes today. Where the hell were you?' *Didn't know they contacted parents. What do I tell her?* 'Well?'

'I was in the park.'

'Why? You like studying, you always have.' *What do I say? Can't tell her the truth, it's too embarrassing.* 'Has something happened?' I don't say anything. 'You'd tell me if it had?'

I murmur, 'Yes.'

'Now I know you don't like your new school much, but you have to soldier on. You can't just bunk off.'

'I have to change school.'

Mum blows air from her nose, and says, 'Didn't want you to go there in the first place. You're stuck there for now though.'

'I want to return to my old school.'

'No chance! You were expelled, remember. You're staying at your school until your GCSEs. Then we'll have a think what to do next. Okay?'

'That's a year away.'

'End of conversation.' She points at me. 'Do not miss any more school!'

I leave the kitchen, go upstairs and take a shower. After scrubbing myself with soap, I shampoo my hair. Can still smell shit. I shampoo my hair again. That smell was far worse than the rotting Antiguan drug dealer. In my room, I lie on the bed with a towel wrapped around my middle and hold up my father's black snakeskin tie. Could wrap it over Dunce's neck like this and pull. No, even better, it's a live black python who obeys my every command. *Throttle Dunce to death. Make it slow.* Nightmare this morning was. The worst moment of my life. Don't want to return to that zoo pretending to be a school. I leap off the bed and throw two left jabs followed by a right cross. Dunce drops to the floor. I kick him. How am I going to get revenge? Dunce and Darragh are the main ones, and that fat sixth former who did the shit. Naming him Dumper.

'Rahh!' I gave my blazer a good wipe in McDonald's, but it could do with a proper clean. I go down to the kitchen. 'Mum.'

'Yes.'

'Want to send my school blazer to the drycleaners.'

'No, you can wear it for another week.'

'But Mum—'

'No!' She stops cutting vegetables, pivots and points a kitchen knife at me. 'Not in the mood for being badgered by you. Did you forget my sister died?' Mum slams the knife into a red pepper. 'Lay the table. We won't need knives, we're having stir-fry. Put out napkins and mats.'

Mum's father has returned to Antigua and my sister is at college. I take two mats and napkins from a drawer. Poison or a nerve agent could work. During midmorning break, I will change into a hazmat suit. The Daggerz gang will all be in the boy's changing room in the basement. I will burst in and spray them with an aerosol can containing a nerve agent. Novichok – that's what the Russians use. They will die slowly. Don't know where to get Novichok though. I pull open the cutlery drawer, grab a fork and jab it at Dunce. *Die!* Then I stab Darragh. And now the fat sixth former, Dumper. I am jabbing the fork repeatedly. Blood is spurting from every member of the gang. Jab, jab, jab. *Die! Die! Die!*

'What're you doing?'

'Nothing.'

'Stop being strange and finish laying the table.'

*

The following morning – I am waiting outside the classroom. Can see through the glass pane in the door that most of the class are already in there, including Dunce. I roll down my sleeve and check the time on my Swatch. It's 09:01. Maths was supposed to start a minute ago, but the teacher hasn't arrived yet. Two boys from my class walk past me and go into the classroom. I knock my forehead against the wall. Only way I'd want to go inside would be if I had a flamethrower. This morning told Mum I wasn't feeling well. She took my temperature. As I didn't have one, she ordered me to go to school. Tried arguing with her but she didn't listen. Just can't face it; think I'll bunk off. Fuck what Mum says. About to walk off when the biology teacher appears.

'What're you doing out here? Get inside.' *Ah!* She opens the classroom door. 'Go on.'

I slink inside with my head bowed and make my way to a desk near the back on the other side of the room to Dunce. I tilt to the side, so I am facing the wall. It's torture being in the same room as that idiot. A bomb in the basement changing room at break time, when the Daggerz gang are in there selling drugs. Will place it under a bench. It will be on a timer. I'll be waiting on the other side of the street. *BOOM!* A great cloud of dust. Bits of brick, debris, and body parts rain down. The top section of a leg drops onto the pavement in front of me. It's thick and muscular, no question it belongs to Darragh. *Splat!* That noise is Dumper's intestines landing on the road. *Smack!* That was Tricia's sister's head landing on the bonnet of a car. Dunce comes stumbling out of the ruined basement, caked in dust and blood. Both his arms have been blown off. He collapses quivering onto the pavement. I stand over him and say, *Eyre. E-Y-R-E.* He won't die until he bleeds out. And the good news is, it'll take a while.

'Smaller organisms have a larger surface area to volume ratio than larger animals … An exchange surface is any part of an organism that allows for the exchange of materials between the organism and its environment. Examples of exchange surfaces in biology include the lungs, skin, and the surfaces of the cells in the gut …'

Dunce has craned his neck forward and is smirking at me. *Ah!* He's laughing. I clench my eyes shut, reach under my desk, and grip onto its front two legs. Biology is over. I am the last to leave the classroom. Tricia is in the corridor blowing a gum bubble. She sucks the gum into her mouth, and says, 'Horatio, are you alright?'

'Yes.'

'Are you sure?'

'I said yes. Your sister is a bitch!'

'Can be, yeah.'

I stomp off. Up ahead, some sixth formers are exiting a classroom used for French. Tricia's sister is there. So is Dumper. I snap the pencil I'm holding in half. And there is Darragh. I pivot around. Tricia's sister calls out, 'Can smell shit.'

Darragh says, 'It's either shit or it's Dior's *parfum de sewage.*'

There is roaring laughter. They'll die for this; every single one of them.

FIVE

IT'S FRIDAY AFTERNOON and I've just got home from school. In my room drinking orange juice and studying French grammar. My week sucked. Since Monday have had no more dealings with the gang, which is something though. Dunce didn't turn up to school today. It was good him not being there, really good. Problem is, he'll likely return on Monday. I grab a pencil off my desk, stab an eraser with it, then leap up and throw a flurry of punches. Dunce falls to the floor. I bend over him and unleash ground and pound. Feeling peckish. There is a multi-pack of salt and vinegar crisps in the kitchen. Will tuck into those. I go downstairs. The kitchen door is closed. Can hear Mum and my sister talking in there. My sister's here for the weekend. There is no point in her going away to college when she's back home every two seconds. About to open the kitchen door when I think I hear Mum say, 'Will.'

It's muffled what with the door being closed. Pretty sure she said that though. I go in. They are sitting at the kitchen table. There are papers on the table. They are both looking up at me. Neither of them says anything. I glance at the papers. Aunt Fatso's address is at the top of one. Below it are numbers with words in capital letters next to them. FUNERAL, WISHES, LEGACIES. It's a will alright. Mum covers the papers with her arms, and says, 'What're you up to?'

'Getting some crisps.'

'Help yourself, they're by the toaster.'

I walk over to the counter, take a packet, and say, 'That's Aunt Fa— Tanice's will.'

Mum doesn't say anything. My sister murmurs, 'Yeah.'

'Why's Shaneeka seeing it, and not me?' Mum snorts, my sister lowers her head. Mum places her elbows on the papers, presses the fingertips of both hands together, and squeezes her eyes shut. 'Mum!' She doesn't respond. 'One of you, tell me.'

Mum opens her eyes, sighs, and says, 'Suppose you might as well find out now.'

She lifts her elbows off the papers. I tilt them towards me and scan them. Under LEGACIES is *I give, subject to inheritance tax my property and its contents, Flat 3 Temple Mansions, RM14 3LQ, London, to Rakesha Robinson.*

I give to Shaneeka Robinson my employee life insurance (Legal & General Ref: 39234ZQA)

I give to Shaneeka Robinson the contents of my bank accounts ...

I am not even mentioned. Fat bitch. I tug on the hair on the sides of my head – 'What about me?'

Mum shakes her head and says, 'There's nothing for you, sorry.'

'Sorry! Shaneeka, how much is the employee life insurance worth?' Her head is still bowed. She doesn't say anything. 'Shaneeka, Mum!'

'Not sure exactly,' murmurs Mum. 'Approximately four years of her salary.'

'Rahh!'

I stomp upstairs and slam my bedroom door shut. Nada, not so much as a family-sized packet of Maltesers. I jump face first onto the bed and bury my face in the duvet. Stay like this for quite a while. Then I roll onto my side. My bedroom floor has turned into a lake of Coca-Cola. Above the lake are hovering Maltesers.

Aunt Fatso is in the lake. She reaches up with a fat arm and tries to grab Maltesers but they hover just out of reach. She is paddling her feet as fast as she can, her arms are above her head, and her hands are grabbing at the Maltesers. But she can't reach them. She slaps her palms together and dives. The Coca-Cola instantly dries up; she plummets to the bedroom floor. I leap out of bed, grab a chainsaw and cut off her arms. It's *Texas Chainsaw Massacre* meets Greek mythology. Blood is spurting everywhere and Aunt Fatso is writhing about like a fish out of water. The gang are here. All of them – Dunce, Darragh, Dumper, and the rest. I rev the chainsaw and race towards them.

'VVVVVVV—'

'Horatio! What're you doing in there?'

*

11:35 – Sunday – I am propped up on one elbow in bed, reading *Bleak House*. Yesterday I went to the boxing gym. Was good letting off steam. Pretended I was giving Aunt Fatso and the gang a good walloping. The bags were their bodies; the pads were their faces. Yesterday my sister said she was so sorry I wasn't left anything in the will. That it was harsh and must be distressing for me. She said this is what happens though if you aren't kind to people and don't show them warmth. She got it the wrong way round. It was Aunt Fatso who bossed me around the whole time. Had to put up with it for years. Forget kind, forget warmth, there should be compensation.

Modern day Tantalus will suffer for eternity for what she did to me. My sister did say she might be prepared to give me a little bit of money to put towards my university expenses, assuming I go to university. Well, it's something I suppose. Not a fat lot though. My sister must be getting two, three hundred grand. All of yesterday I was pissed off about it, and the bog flush. Other than the boxing gym and watching a few hours of television, I spent the rest of the day in my room. My sister is calling me. She is clearing the back garden while Mum sorts out stuff at her new flat, Aunt Fatso's old flat. Was Mum and my sister's idea to clear the garden. Hasn't been done since we moved here when I was a baby. Don't really want to get involved, but my sister said she will buy me takeaway for lunch if I help. Will be Five Guys, Deliveroo deliver it. Bet she opts for something healthy, like sushi or salad.

'Horatio, come on!'

When I step into the garden, she says, 'Can you take the bags out?'

There are two bin liners on the patio with earth and bits of brick in. She has got a fair bit done. The bin liners have been doubled up and not filled too much. Not a bad idea, as would be a disaster if they broke when they are being carried through the house. Quite clever my sister is. Of course, she's related to me. I pick up the bin liners, lug them through the house and dump them beside the wheelie bins by the front gate. There isn't enough room for them in the wheelie bins. My sister said we'll take the gardening rubbish up to the dump in the car later. The street is empty, I can't see a single person. It's unusually quiet. I go inside and close the door. My phone is ringing. It's Serena.

'Hello.'

'Hi gorgeous, what're you up to?'

'Clearing the back garden.'

'You do the most boring stuff.'

'Wasn't my idea.'

'What're you up to later?'

'As in when?'

'Sixish. A friend is coming over. Join us. We'll have pizza, get stoned, play *Gran Turismo*. Will kick your ass at it.'

'Dream on.'

'Just you wait. You up for it?'

'Yeah.'

'Awesome. Bring a bit of skunk with you, my friend will buy some.'

'Sure. Bye.'

My sister is pulling weeds from between the paving stones. I will remove the dead thorny bushy next to the wall. Where are the secateurs? There they are. I snip branches off the dead bush and shove them in a bin liner.

'Was so lovely seeing Granddad. Pity he had to leave so soon.' *This bush should've been removed years ago. Mum has done absolutely nothing in the garden.* 'You haven't seen you know who, have you?' *Rat!* 'Pretty sure it was him I saw when I was with Grandad. Freaked me out.' *Prickly this bush is.* 'If either of us see him again, we'll have to tell Mum. I'm going to get a glass of water. Do you want some?'

'I'm good.'

God knows what Rat's up to. Was he satisfied with throwing a brick through the window? I'm thinking he's not done yet. After all he went to prison because of me, and I killed his friend. Thorny this stalk is. I hold it by the tip and drop it in the bin liner. Nearly there. Can reach the main stem now. I crouch down and sever it at the bottom close to the ground. About to pick it up when I notice a green object sticking out from a hole near the bottom of the garden wall, where a brick is missing. Why the hell is it here? I pick it up. It's a green metallic box with an inscription of a fish on the lid. Whoever put this here, was hiding it for some reason. I rattle the box. There's stuff inside. Mysterious, it could be something valuable. I put the box down on the ground, as don't want my sister seeing it, in case there's something valuable inside. I pick up the severed stalk, cut it up into smaller lengths and drop the bits in the bin liner.

'Can you come and help me with these weeds.' I shove the bin liner on top of the box, go to the rear of the garden and help my sister with the weeds. Who left the box there? And why did they hide it? My sister takes off her gardening gloves. 'After lunch we'll power hose the paving stones. Then we're done until we get topsoil for the flowerbeds.' She walks through the garden and goes into the kitchen. I pick up the box. It's too big for the pocket of my shorts, so I stuff it in the waistband, pull my T-shirt over it, and go inside. My sister is in the kitchen leaning on a counter, fiddling with her phone. I hurry through the kitchen. 'You haven't even told me what you want for lunch.'

'Five Guys. Bacon cheeseburger, small fries. For toppings, lettuce, mustard, grilled onions, tomato, relish.'

'Slow down.'

I repeat my order; she jots it on a piece of paper. I jog upstairs to my bedroom, push the door closed, pull out the box, dump myself on a chair, put the box on the desk, and open it. There are loads of things inside. I empty them onto the desk. There is a silver crucifix necklace, a gold earring, a monocle, and a silver signet ring. These could be valuable. And there's more. This looks like a tooth. It is a tooth – a gold-capped molar. And there are two more objects – a braided blonde pigtail and a dreadlock. Can understand why someone might keep jewellery in here. But why would there be hair and a tooth? And why would the box be hidden in my garden? And why did whoever hid it there not come to collect it? They obviously wanted to keep these things. Stands to reason they couldn't return for it. How long has this box been in my garden for? None of it makes sense.

Having attached the crucifix necklace around my neck, I put the signet ring on the little finger of my left hand. Can't put the gold earring on, as don't have pierced ears. Don't want them either. I pick up the gold-capped tooth. These four items could be described as bling. This monocle isn't bling though; it's the opposite of bling. Old-fashioned, sort of academic looking. No one wears monocles these days. The two locks of hair are bizarre. Who would keep a pigtail and a dreadlock? I pick up the tooth, recline in the chair and watch the light reflecting off it. Fool's Gold had a gold-capped tooth. His though was a front tooth, an incisor. If this collection was all jewellery, I would assume it had been stolen and that's why it was hidden. But there's this tooth and the hair.

While I've lived here, it is highly unlikely anyone would have hidden that box in the garden wall. Could have been hidden there before I moved here. However, the garden was presumably cleared at some point, and it would have been found. Besides, whoever left it there would have returned for it, unless something happened to them. I put the tooth down and tap my fingertips against the desk ...

My father! He was shot when I was five. Could he have hidden it in the wall? I know he didn't live here, but he must've visited me, and presumably went in the garden. Could well have been in some sort of trouble. After all my father ended up getting shot. Him being shot could have been the result, the, ah, culmination of something. Whatever was happening to him could explain why he hid the box there. He was planning to return for it when things calmed down. Why would he have all these things though? And why would he want to hide them ...? Didn't want anyone else finding them obviously. If it was him who hid the box. My father may never have even been in the garden. *Ding dong* – that was the doorbell. This is bizarre, none of it makes sense. First step is to ask Mum.

'Horatio!' I put everything inside the box, put the box in a desk drawer, and go downstairs to the kitchen. 'Food's here. Didn't you hear the doorbell?'

'I heard it.'

She takes a container of sushi and chopsticks from a bag and puts them on the table. I take my Five Guys out of the bag and unwrap the burger.

'Feel free to say thank you at any point.'

'Thank you.' I have a bite of my burger and chew on it. Wait a second, my sister will know about my father. She's older than me and should remember if he came here. Maybe she even saw him in the garden. 'Shaneeka.'

'Yes.'

'Do you remember my father visiting here?'

She lowers her chopsticks and says, 'Random question, what brought that on?'

'Well, do you?'

'Um.' She stirs wasabi into a bowl of soy sauce. 'Yeah, I do.' She looks up at me. 'All I can remember is coming out of the living room and seeing him at the front door. Mum was angry with him; she was telling him off. Don't know why. Then he came inside.'

'That's all you remember?'

'Yes. Why?'

'No reason.'

'There must be a reason, or you wouldn't have asked.' I don't reply. 'How's your burger?'

'Good.'

My sister dips a piece of sushi in the bowl of soy sauce, then raises it to her mouth. I chew on a mouthful of fries. It's a collection of some sort; there is no other explanation. Has to be. Can hear a key turning in the front door. Mum comes into the kitchen and dumps her handbag on the table.

'Traffic was awful, took ages to get here. You two look like you're having a nice lunch.'

Am about to ask Mum about my father when my sister says, 'Mum, look at the garden.'

Mum opens the door to the garden – 'Looks much tidier. Well done you two.'

My sister says, 'Just have the power hosing to do. We'll do it after lunch.'

'Mum.'

'Yes, darling.'

'Did my father ever go in the garden?'

She withdraws her head, closes the door, squints at me, and says, 'Um, yeah, he did. Used to play cricket with you in the garden.' *Interesting.* 'With the mini cricket bat he gave you.' She sits down. 'He even draped a net between the walls to stop the ball going into the neighbours' gardens. You were only five, can't imagine you would have hit the ball hard enough for it go over the wall. Why are you asking?'

'Was wondering because I've been in the garden all day.'

'Oh, okay.' She turns to my sister. 'The flat is looking pretty tidy now. I gave it a good clean. A-hh, can't bring myself to go through her things.'

'So don't until you feel up to it. There's no rush.'

*

The next day – I'm in English. Yesterday afternoon, I searched for the box online. Found an identical one for sale on *eBay*. It is a fly-fishing tin. That's why there's a picture of a fish on it. Was described on *eBay* as retro. This model was sold in the nineteen-seventies and early eighties. My father could well have been given it as a present when he was a child. It's the kind of thing someone might have given a kid in those days. My father kept it his whole life and used it for his collection. If it was only jewellery in there, would assume it was stolen and that's why he hid it. From the news articles online relating to my father's death, I know the police think he shot the man dead who shot him. They shot each other. Seems logical the seven things in the fly-fishing tin used to belong to other people my father—

'Horatio, read for us.'

Where are we? The Bangladeshi girl leans across the aisle and points at a paragraph halfway down the page. I stand up and read – 'I would fain exercise some better faculty than that of fierce speaking; fain find nourishment for some less fiendish feeling than that of sombre indignation …'

I stop reading and sit down. At a desk two to my left, Tricia is blowing me a kiss. At the desk next to her, Dunce is leaning forward with his head tilted towards me. He drags his right index finger across his throat. It'll be his throat that will be slit, not mine. Just have to figure out how. The teacher tells Tricia to read. She spits her chewing gum on her desk and stands up.

'Bessie's presence, compared with the thoughts over which I had been brooding, seemed cheerful; even though, as usual, she was somewhat cross.' Tricia is putting on a posh voice. 'The fact is, after my conflict with and victory over Mrs. Reed, I was not disposed to care much for the nursemaid's transitory anger ...'

Yesterday, after researching the fly-fishing tin, I kept thinking about the items in it. Found out online some serial killers keep mementos of their victims. This is to remind them of their kills. Serial killers like to ... reminisce, that's the word, on what they did, what they achieved. When they're with the object, they remember the kill. This is why my father kept all those things in the fly-fishing tin. They were mementos. Feel quite sure of it. It's the only possible explanation for the gold-capped tooth, dreadlock, and pigtail. There's this expression – like father, like son. He was a killer, same as me.

Why didn't I take a memento from Fool's Gold and the Antiguan drug dealer? Because didn't know I was supposed to. I slam my fist on the desk. The teacher says, 'Horatio, why did you do that?'

'Cos he's a wanker,' says Dunce.

'Wasn't asking you. And don't use that language in my class. Horatio?'

'No reason.'

I crane my neck forward and glance to my left. What memento will I get off him? There's nothing obvious, that's for sure. Could always take a tooth. The bell goes and everyone rushes for the door. In the corridor, Tricia strokes my shoulder, and says, 'Why're you so angry? Surely not still cos of the bog flush.' She blows a chewing gum bubble. It bursts and she sucks the gum into her mouth. 'Shit happens, let it go. That's what my mum always says to me. She's into yoga.'

When I enter the chemistry classroom, Dunce is holding the

little finger of his right hand horizontally at the bottom of his left index finger. That's the Daggerz gang sign. I sit on the other side of the classroom, as far away from the idiot as possible. To be classified a serial killer, you have to have three kills. I am only one away from achieving that feat. My father killed seven people I know of, well eight actually. There was also the Albanian in the flat. As they shot each other, my father wasn't able to get a memento off him.

The teacher is talking about noble gases. Known all about them since I was seven or eight. I want to kill the whole gang, the main members anyway. Would be fun to hunt them down one by one. I'm leaning towards Dunce first, as can't bear to share a classroom with him. However, logistically it should probably all be done at once. A bomb, gas, shooting. There's a term for people who kill loads of people at once. Mass murderers is what they call them, not serial killers. And then there's Rat. He could do with being killed as well. There are too many to kill. I knock my fists together. The teacher says, 'Horatio?'

'Yeah.'

'Tell us, which is the most radioactive of the noble gases?'

'Radon.'

*

School has just ended and I am waiting around a corner for Bart. I'm getting more skunk from the estate. Run out and Serena wants some for her friends. Seeing her after school tomorrow. Mum is at work, so she won't notice if I'm a bit late. Where is he? Hurry up. Would rather go without him as Bart takes twenty quid in commission, money that's coming out of my pocket. However, the C-Crew wouldn't let me into the building without him because they don't know me. So that's just the way it is, for now anyway. Here he comes. It's the same procedure as last time. We take off our school blazers, he speaks to them on the intercom, they let us in, and we go up to the top floor.

The boss of the C-Crew is slouched on a chair with a PlayStation 5 controller gripped in his hands. Three teenagers – two girls and a boy are on a sofa. The boy is also holding a PlayStation controller. They don't even acknowledge we're here. It's football, *FIFA*. This is probably the most popular game there is. I don't like football, and fortunately neither does Serena. The two girls and the boy are wearing green tracksuits, the uniform of the C-Crew. The boss is wearing green tracksuit bottoms and a white T-shirt with a gold chain hanging over it. The chain has a big circular medallion that looks like a large gold coin. He shouts, 'GOAL!' and wags his right index and middle fingers in the air.

The other gang members clap. The girl says 'Sick', and one of the boys, 'Wicked volley.'

When the boss twists his head towards us, Bart claps a couple of times. The boss barks, 'Show some respect!'

The same girl says, 'Clap, tosser.'

I clap my hands. The boss says, 'What're you after?'

Bart says, 'An oz.'

The boss clicks his fingers and the girl clambers off the sofa and gets a polythene-wrapped lump of skunk. She chucks it at Bart, who catches it. I take the money from my mini rucksack. Bart takes a twenty-pound note and I give the rest to the girl, who counts it. The amount looks spot on. I put it in my mini rucksack. The boss says, 'Not so much as a squeak from the Daggerz.' I clench my fists. 'Running scared, pussies.' *I will kill them all.* 'What you looking so stressed for? Yeah, you!' He is pointing at me with the PlayStation controller. 'You're scared of the cunts.'

'No! But I hate them, they're idiots.'

'Yeah. Can't do nothing about 'em though can you.' *I can; I will.* He is grinning. That gold chain and medallion would make an excellent memento. 'Stop staring at me twat and fuck off.' I turn around. 'Tell 'em faggot Daggerz, Bad Dog is coming for 'em.'

Tell them yourself, imbecile.

*

The following evening – The two cars are scooting around the circuit at high speed. Serena is driving a Bugatti, her friend a Porsche. I am sandwiched between them on the sofa. When Serena veers to the left, her silky blonde hair strokes my cheek. There is only one lap to go, and they are neck and neck. I rest the back of my head on the sofa and look up at the ceiling. It's as if I'm a reincarnation of my father. We're the same. One of his mementos was a gold-capped tooth. My first kill also had a gold-capped tooth. Well, fool's gold, as he couldn't afford real gold. Similar though, really similar. And there's a dreadlock in the fly-fishing tin. My second kill, the drug dealer in Antigua, had dreadlocks, stumpy ones.

'It's gone horribly wrong!'

That was Serena's friend. The Porsche has come off at a corner and spun. Serena shoots across the finish line, punches the air, and shrieks, 'WOAH!'

'Epic race,' says her friend.

'Intense,' says Serena.

'Let's have a joint,' says her friend.

'Yeah,' says Serena. 'Can't have it in the garden though. A neighbour complained to my mum last time I smoked out there. I blamed it on the girl who lives next door. Told my mum I had smelt a weird smell coming from there a few times. Think my mum believed me cos the girl's a Jehovah's Witness. All the family are. Mum said Jehovah's Witness kids rebel against their upbringing. Anyway, means we have to smoke it in the park. Get a move on and make it.'

'I'm on it,' says her friend.

Serena's mother had to rush to the garage, as she has a flat tyre. My father knew that one day I would find his fly-fishing tin, and that I would understand what the contents were.

'Horatio,' says Serena. 'What's up with you today?'

'Nothing.'

'You seem spaced out. Are you stoned?'

'No.'

'So, wake up then and participate. You are with two hot girls; you should be happy.' She perches herself on my lap and kisses me on the cheek. 'I'd be stressing out a little bit too if I were you. I'm going to whoop your ass in *Gran Turismo*.'

Not happening. Her friend says, 'Serena, you sounded so American when you said that.'

'*Hello*, I am half American. My father's from America. Hurry up with that joint.'

We go to the park, to the same spot behind the skateboard ramp in the conservation area. Then we return to Serena's house, eat Monster Munch, drink Pepsi, and play PlayStation. I easily beat Serena at *Gran Turismo*. She gets angry because it's her game. After smacking me with a cushion, she leaps on top of me and tries to smother me with it. I laugh. Her friend jumps on me too. I play *Gran Turismo* with the friend. It's quite a close race until the last circuit when she comes off the track and spins, same as she did in her race with Serena. I leave.

Just got off the bus. On the walk home, I think about my father. He must have had a lot of fun killing all those people. He was smart too, to get away with it for so long. It's a pity he ended up getting shot. Otherwise, we could have been a father and son serial killer team. I don't want to go to school tomorrow. Never felt like this at my old schools. Wasn't that I wanted to go, but I didn't dread going. My school sucks bigtime. I kick an empty beer can across the pavement, cross the road and take my housekey from the pocket of my trousers.

When I look up, I see the word *Murderer* has been painted in red paint on the front garden's wall. *Rat!* How dare he do this? The shops will be closed, so can't buy anything to take it off with. And even if one was open, Mum is expecting me back now. She texted me to say she was putting a pizza in the oven and to come straight home. If Mum had seen it, she probably would have phoned me, not just sent the text. Rat must've sprayed it when she was in the house. What do I do?

Mum won't be leaving the house again today, which means she won't even notice it until tomorrow. The neighbours might though. I need to cover it up. The two dustbins on the paving stones in the front garden will do. I drag them through the gate and position them on the pavement, blocking the graffiti. Fair chance Mum won't even notice they've been moved. When she goes to work in the morning, she turns left out of the front gate, and the dustbins will be on the right. Fingers crossed she's still half asleep and doesn't notice. I go inside. Mum is in the kitchen.

'Did you have fun at Serena's?'

'Yeah.'

'What did you do there?'

'Played PlayStation, ate Monster Munch, drunk Pepsi. Her friend was there too.'

'Had a fun time then from the sound of things.' She opens the oven door. 'Pizza is almost ready.'

Good, Mum's not aware of the graffiti. If she was, she would have said something straight away.

SIX

THE NEXT DAY – I'm in chemistry, the last class of the day. Dunce is at a desk two behind mine. Don't want to be this close to him. However, I was the last to arrive, and this was the only desk available. Either he dies, or I move school. Simple as that. Even if I went to a new school, I would return to get revenge on him. The periodic table is on a screen at the front of the classroom. If I was at a proper school like I used to go to, it would be interesting studying the periodic table. But with Dunce in my class, studying anything is a nightmare.

'Actinides, or the actinoid series as they are sometimes referred to, comprise fifteen metallic chemical elements.' The teacher taps his ruler on the line of elements marked in brown at the bottom of the periodic table. 'Their atomic numbers run from eighty-nine to one hundred and three.'

'Horatio.' That was Dunce. I grit my teeth. 'The elements yeah, are the same colour as what was in your hair the other day.'

I grip the sides of my desk. The girl on my right nudges me and whispers, 'What's he on about?'

I shrug my shoulders.

'The most famous actinide, or should I say infamous, is this one.' The teacher taps his ruler on the element, PU. 'Plutonium is the element with the highest atomic number to occur in nature ...'

'Looks well different your hair does,' says a boy gang member. 'From how it looked in the bogs the other day.'

I clench my fists. Again, the girl next to me says, 'What's he on about?'

'Don't know.'

'Bog Boy.' *Dunce.* 'HIHIHI …!'

Die!

'What's so funny?' says the teacher. 'Care to share it with the class.'

'HIHIHI …' I will grab a sharpened pencil from my pencil case, race over to him, stab it through his eye and embed it in his pea brain. Instead, I squeeze my eyes shut and grip the sides of my desk. 'HIHI …!'

'Stop laughing!'

'HIHI …'

'Dalton, get out!'

'Nah, done nah. Stayin' put.'

'I said get out.' The teacher is pointing at Dunce with a ruler. 'Go!'

'You deaf? Said I'm stayin' put.'

'We'll see about that.'

The teacher leaves the classroom. Everyone starts talking. Dunce says, 'Teacher's pissin' me off. Keeps it up, we should drag him down the khazis. HIHI!'

Tricia says, 'Then you'll be suspended again.'

'Yeah,' says Dunce. 'But fuck it, would be a laugh, innit?'

The science teacher comes into the classroom with two other male teachers. He says, 'Dalton, get out.'

'Fuckin' hell!' Dunce stands up. 'What is it with you lot?' He marches out. 'Teachers, wankers!'

No more Dunce for today. The remaining twenty minutes of this class are going to be bliss. Why can't it be like this all the time? While the teacher talks about the actinoid series, I wonder what memento Dunce will yield to me. Yield – great word. There is nothing screaming memento I've ever seen him with. Could always take a button from his clothes, I suppose. But how am I going to kill Dunce? It would be impossible at school. Could follow him home and creep into his house. That's not going to be easy; it might well be impossible. For one thing his big brother will probably be there. And how will I kill him, and all the others who humiliated me? I scrunch up a piece of paper. The girl next to me leans across the aisle and asks me why I'm stressing out. I tell her to mind her own business. The class is nearly over. I need to go to the shops and find something to remove Rat's graffiti with before Mum gets home from work.

*

It's six-twenty, and I'm in my room with my mementos spread out on the desk in front of me. Mum will be back soon. Wouldn't want her walking in and seeing all these. I'll hear her though. And besides she always knocks on my door, doesn't just burst in. Well, Mum might if she was angry. But she has no reason to be. The hardware shop I went to on the way home recommended paint thinner for removing graffiti. Bought the smallest container of it they had. Good news was the graffiti came off easily. Maybe because Rat didn't use proper spray paint. Was surprised he spelled murderer correctly. He must've looked it up. I recline in my chair, put my hands behind my head and interlock the fingers. Rat will be running out of ideas by now. He's not the most imaginative, and he is thick as shit. That's why he was best friends with moron Fool's Gold. Stupid as he is, Rat must realise that by targeting me and my family's house, he is risking getting in trouble with the police, again.

Surely, he doesn't want that. The graffiti could, should, be the end of it. But that's not to say it is. I pick the gold-capped molar off the desk and rotate it in my fingertips. Chances are it belonged to a loser not dissimilar to Fool's Gold. There are a fair few losers, wannabe gangsters like Fool's Gold out there with gold-capped teeth, or in his case fool's gold-capped. Any normal person would ask their dentist for a cap the same colour as their tooth. Enamel is what they use. Seemingly, idiots opting for gold and fool's gold-capped teeth run the risk of being murdered by serial killers. Have two examples to prove it. My bet is there are a load more out there. Dentists should be warning these imbeciles when they ask for gold. *Yes, we can do that for you. However, you are aware I assume you will look like a twat. You will also be five times more likely to be murdered by a serial killer and have your gold-capped tooth taken as a memento.*

'HA, HA HAHAHA!'

I can hear Mum downstairs. Must've been laughing so loudly, I didn't hear the front door. I put the mementos in the fly-fishing tin and stick it to the underside of my chest of drawers with tape. This is where I'm keeping it from now on in. Would be bad if Mum ever found it. She won't if it's here. Wonder what's for dinner. I go down to the kitchen. Mum says, 'Hey, how was your day?'

'So, so.'

'What were you laughing at?'

'Something funny I saw. A meme.'

'Must've been funny, you were laughing loudly.' She pours water into a glass. 'When I left for work, our bins were on the pavement. Did you put them there?'

'Yes.'

'Why?'

'Because I thought it was bin day today.'

'Bin day is Friday. Thanks for thinking of it though.'

Good thing Mum didn't move the bins. Was probably in a rush to get to work, or just couldn't be bothered.

*

09:36 – The following day – I am in the second class of the day, French. The teacher says, *'Répétez après moi. Non, pas du tout.'*

'Non, pas du tout,' repeat the class.

Well, some of them anyway. Most of them have terrible accents. The *T* at the end of tout is supposed to be silent. The teacher says, *'Répétez après moi—'*

Tricia shouts, 'Check out this mad chicken dance on *TikTok*!'

The teacher groans. Near on everyone rushes over to her desk, other than me, the Dinka, the Bangladeshi girl, and the boy with the crooked legs who can't walk properly. The teacher calls out, 'Return to your desks.'

'Hold your horses,' says Tricia. '*Chevaux*, in't they in French? Horses.'

Some of the pupils are laughing; some of them are doing a chicken dance. This school is an embarrassment. The bell goes. The next class is PE. There are two PE classes a week. It's the only exercise slash sport offered here. Tricia is walking next to me along the corridor. She flicks a length of dirty looking blonde hair off her wide forehead.

'You're fit.'

Tricia is not worth one-hundredth of Serena. She strokes my arm and jogs away.

'Oi, Bog Boy!'

Ah, Dunce. He's behind me. Gob lands on the floor beside me. Disgusting. Will kill him. I slip into a classroom and wait. Don't want to go in the changing rooms, as he'll be in there. So, I stay in the corridor and wait for him to leave. Bart comes out of the changing rooms in his PE kit. He says, 'Wouldn't be going in there if I were you. Dunce is pissed off with you and he's mouthing off. He's jealous Tricia likes you. Fuck knows why, bog standard she is. If that.'

Sub bog standard is what she is. I get changed in the corridor. Pull my PE shorts over my boxer shorts, as don't want to be seen naked. Some girls come out of the girls changing room. One of them wolf whistles at me.

We are doing basketball drills. I am dribbling a basketball around cones when Dunce struts in. The PE teacher says, 'You're late!'

'Yeah.'

He picks up a basketball, glares at me, and spits on the floor. *Animal.* After doing a few drills, the boys split into two teams, as do the girls. Dunce is on the opposing team. The girls are going first, as there's not enough space for us all to play at once. The Dinka is scoring non-stop. She's tall, over six foot, and sort of floats around the court. The teacher yells, 'Spectacular play, Yeno!'

A boy says, 'Fit Yeno is. Would knock her.'

'Nah,' says another boy. 'Not into black birds.'

'That's racist.'

'It's not. They just don't float my boat.'

Dunce is watching me. He does resemble a bull terrier. He's stocky, ugly, and has small pointed ears. How dare he, they, bog flush me? Worst moment of my life that was. I close my eyes and knock my forehead against the wall. Need to get revenge; I must get revenge. A boy nudges me.

'What you headbutting the wall for?'

I stop doing it. It's time for the boys' match. Haven't played basketball much, but I'm good at it. I pass the ball up field and Bart slam dunks. Everyone is whooping and clapping. The teacher punches the air. Bart is a stoner and comes across as slow. However, he is amazing at basketball. Not surprising, as he's six foot seven. I might have the best player on my team, but the other team are winning. The bull terrier, Dunce, is dribbling up the court. He isn't good at basketball like everything else. He's tenacious though. Dunce is giving the ball to the better and taller players to score the points. He barges into me, and spits, 'Wanker.'

'Dunce.'

'What's that, tosser?'

'Language Dalton!' calls out the teacher. 'Do it again, you're off.'

Dunce spits on the floor ... The ten second clapper has just gone, and my team is two points down. The ball bounces off my team's net's rim. There is a scramble for the ball. Bart catches it and hurls it up the court to me. I dribble forward. In front of me are two opposing players, and hurtling towards me from my right is Dunce. The whistle is about to go. Have to go for the three points. I shoot. The ball goes through the net. Dunce barges into my side; I topple to the floor. Will kill him. I clamber up and shove him in the chest. The teacher drags him away. As I step towards him, Bart grabs my arms.

'Chill. He is a sore loser.'

I stamp the floor. Dinka gives me a thumbs up. Tricia says, 'Nice shot, Horatio.'

I take a deep breath through my nose. Dunce wrests himself free from the teacher and stomps out of the hall.

Morning classes are over, and I am in the dining hall, eating an apple at a table with some of my classmates. At another table full of sixth formers, can see Dunce talking to his big brother. Is he complaining about me? A girl from my class nudges me with her elbow.

'Horatio, you look well nervous. What's happened?'

'Nothing!'

'Alright, no need to bite my head off.'

Dunce is stomping off. On the way out of the dining room, he punches the wall. A good sign. Finishing off a second apple when Tricia comes over and plunks herself down next to me. *Go away!*

'Dalton was whinging about you to his big bruver. Thought he'd be up for bog flushing you again, or something.' *Ah!* 'Darragh wasn't up for it. He told little bruver to deal with you himself. Dalton's having a hissy fit, being a big baby.'

Excellent. Dunce is pretty harmless without his big brother.

*

It's 19:03, and I have just finished my homework. It was geography and maths. Geography was writing a passage about upland Britain. These parts of the country feature U-shaped valleys and eroded mountain peaks. From now on in, students are going to be able to get AI to do their homework for them. My homework is so easy, I wouldn't be tempted to. Even if was difficult, I'd want to do it myself. Maths homework was ratios. Basic stuff the average nine-year-old could do.

Mum's back from work. She's been on the phone with my sister. Think she's making dinner now. It's stir-fry. These days Mum is always cooking stir-fry. Probably because it takes next to no time to prepare and is quite healthy. I will spend some time with my mementos. I get down on my knees, reach under the chest of drawers, remove the tape, pull out the fly-fishing tin, and empty the contents on my bed. This could have been a drug dealer's dreadlock. The drug dealer I shot in Antigua had dreadlocks, stumpy ones. This drug dealer might have been getting on my father's nerves, or maybe it was an opportunistic kill, same as with the one I shot. Then again maybe this dreadlock was worn by an alternative colleague at the council my father worked at. He was a big pain in the arse, so my father eradicated him.

Intriguing this blonde pigtail is. Women don't normally wear their hair in this style. My guess is this was a child or teenager's hair. Either that or a girly woman. A really annoying one who pissed off my father bigtime. Hitting women is seen as bad, and my father had style. Can tell that from the suits and ties he left me. No way he would have hit her. Shot, strangled, poisoned, pushed into an oncoming car, train, or off something high, is what I'm thinking.

I've only killed men so far. And for the most part it's males I want to kill. Dunce, Darragh, Dumper, Rat. Could count the number of women I'd like to kill on one hand. First up, would be the therapist Mum sent me to after I got expelled from my old school. The patronising bitch caused problems for me, well tried to anyway. Then there's Mum's father's wife, Genevieve. Nightmare in Antigua that bossy cow was. Would get it for sure. Aunt Fatso was bossy too. And she left me nothing. Deserves to stew for eternity in the Coca-Cola lake with the Maltesers hovering out of reach. Modern day Tantalus. *Ha,* like that. There's also Tricia's sister. She pissed me off by stripping off my blazer and shirt in the toilets. Would knock her off if I got a chance.

SEVEN

THE FOLLOWING EVENING – I am at the boxing gym. The instructor calls out, 'Jab, jab, right cross, left hook.'

The class does the combo. We repeat it loads of times. Then we move on to pads and bags. Currently, I am hitting a heavy bag. Jab, right cross to the body, left hook to the liver. And quicker – Jab, right cross, left hook. The bag transforms into Dunce. My jab lands on the tip of his nose, the right cross in his solar plexus, and the left hook to the liver drops him to the floor. I grab an axe, behead him with a single swipe, stand over the body, and say, *Jane Eyre. Eyre, as in E-Y-R-E.* Blood is spurting everywhere. I am looking down at the corpse, wondering what I'm going to take for a memento.

'Oi, you!' That's the trainer. He's talking to me. 'Stop staring at the floor and get to work.'

I resume hitting the bag. Next up is the gang's boss, Darragh. He's big, so I don't stay in front of him and trade punches. Instead, I stand on the balls of my feet, keep on the move, dodge his punches, pepper him with light punches to the head, and dig hard punches to the body. This is taking a toll on what they call in the gym, a gas tank. Darragh's getting tired and his punches are laboured. Can see them coming a mile away. A punch to both kidneys should do it. *Bam, bam* – he's down on one knee. Where's the axe?

'That's us for today. Good effort girls and boys.'

I am drenched with sweat. Haven't been this sweaty since Antigua. After downing a load of water, I dry myself with a towel in the changing rooms, get changed, walk to the bus stop, and get on the bus. It's only two stops from here to the bus stop closest to my house. My phone is ringing. It's Serena.

'*Hi*. What's up?'

'On my way home from the gym.'

'What were you doing in the gym?'

'Boxing.'

'Cool. I had a Spanish lesson this evening with my tutor online. Have one lesson a week after school. People are here for dinner, boring people, Mum's friends. They're asking non-stop questions about school. Want to get stoned so bad. By the way, I've been practising *Gran Turismo*. Will kick your ass next time.'

'*Ha*, never going to happen.'

'That's what you think. You're not into *TikTok*, are you?'

'No.'

'Why not? It's awesome.'

'It's not my thing. It's annoying. At school, a girl showed the class a chicken dance on *TikTok*. They were laughing and some of them were dancing a chicken dance. It's so childish.'

'*Hello*, that's one clip. *TikTok* has millions, maybe tens of millions of videos on it. Mum's calling me. Got to return to the boring guests. Bye.'

She hangs up. This is my stop. I get off the bus. It is starting to get dark. The pavement is heaving with people and there is lots of traffic on the road. A gaggle of people are laughing and shouting. Raucous is how their behaviour would be described. They're drunk, no doubt. There is a pub on the corner. The walk home will take approximately six minutes. I turn off the main road and walk down a residential street. A Deliveroo scooter darts past me from the opposite direction. Might be delivering Five Guys, or maybe pizza. Could do with either of those right now. Had some risotto Mum made before I left for boxing. Mum is not much of a cook, but she is alright at making risottos. It had prawns in it. Well, more shrimps than prawns. There was loads left, will have some when I get home. Can hear running feet behind me. I look over my shoulder. A jogger wearing a pink fluorescent jacket is coming this way. They jog past me.

The streetlights switch on. I pass a council block then walk past a row of railings running along the side of small park. Dance music is blaring from a car. Another scooter drives past. I go around the corner. Only two streets away from home now. It is quiet, unusually so for London. This street seems to be totally deserted. Am about to turn into my street when I hear footsteps close behind me. I am swivelling around when something hard smashes into the side of my head. I collapse to my knees. Someone is standing over me with a hammer raised at shoulder height. The hammer descends and hits me in the head. Stars appear. I topple face first onto the pavement. Everything goes black.

*

I awaken in a bed. It's not my bed. Where am I? Try hauling myself up to a sitting position, but there's a jolt of pain in my head, and I collapse onto the mattress. *Ahh*, worse than any headache this. I close my eyes and take deep breaths through my nose. After a while the pain reduces to a dull throb. I open my eyes. The walls are blue, same colour as the pillow. On my right, there is a thin table on wheels. Can feel something sticking into my left forearm. It's a drip. It is hanging from a stand beside the bed. Why am I in hospital? *Ow*, my head is hurting. I raise my right hand to my head. There are bandages on it. What happened to me? Can remember being at boxing class, travelling on the bus, speaking to Serena on the phone. Then nothing; it's a blank. Did a car drive into me? A nurse comes into the room.

'You're awake. How are you feeling?'

'Bad.'

'Arrr.' She strokes my arm. 'Poor you.'

'Where am I?'

'You're in hospital.'

'Obviously. Which hospital?'

'The Mordant.'

Same hospital Aunt Fatso was in. When the nurse presses a button on a control panel attached to the bed, I rise to a sitting position. She pulls the wheeled table across the bed and puts a glass of water on it. I have a sip.

'Why am I here?'

'You hurt your head.'

'Know that. There are bandages around it. What happened to me?'

'The doctor will see you soon.'

'What happened, I said?'

The nurse leaves. *Ow*, my head is pounding. All that talking didn't help. Should've asked the nurse for painkillers, not Nurofen, something strong like morphine. Still can't remember anything after speaking to Serena. Did I get off the bus and get hit by a car? Unlikely, I am always careful crossing the road. Did a drunk driver come onto the pavement and knock me over? All this thinking is making my head hurt more.

This room is exactly the same as the one Aunt Fatso was in. Only difference is there aren't any Lindt Lindor milk chocolate truffles in here. No bad thing, as feeling a bit queasy, and those things are sickly. Would probably end up spewing if I ate any. Might be feeling queasy because I was under anaesthetic, or maybe because of the medication they've given me. My head is throbbing and I'm feeling very tired. I press the down button on the control panel; the bed lowers to a horizontal position. The more I try to remember what happened to me, the more my head hurts.

I have just woken up. Mum's here. She comes over to the bed and kisses my cheek.

'You're awake. How are you feeling?'

'Groggy.'

I press the up button on the control panel. Mum says, 'Thought I'd seen the last of this place.'

'You were wrong.'

'Sure was.'

'What happened to me? Was I hit by a car?'

'No darling, that's not what happened.'

'What happened?' My head is throbbing. 'Ow!'

'Are you okay?'

'No, my head hurts.'

Mum places her hand on my shoulder, and says, 'Try and relax.'

'What happened to me?'

'Ah, you were—'

There is a knock on the door. It opens. A woman with a stethoscope comes in, bends over the bed, and says, 'How're you feeling?'

'Bad.'

She smiles. Nothing funny about it. She steps away from the bed, and says, 'You've suffered trauma to your brain, so it's not surprising.'

'Will I be alright?'

'All signs so far are positive. You have some fractures to your skull though.'

That's not good. 'What will happen to me?'

'You'll be kept here for observation. As I said, the signs so far are positive. We'll give you another scan soon.'

'Ow!'

I clutch my head. The doctor says, 'Take it easy. The nurse will bring you some painkillers.'

She leaves the room. Mum follows her out. Damn, I wanted to

ask her what happened to me. Why is no one telling me? *Ah*, and why can't I remember? *Ow!* My head is pounding. Nurse, hurry up. Mum and the nurse come back in. The nurse gives me two pills. These pills are big, which is promising. She is talking with Mum. You've given me the pills nurse, now go away, I want to talk to my mother. They are still talking. I close my eyes and wait. Finally, they've stopped. When I hear the door close, I open my eyes.

'What happened to me?'

Mum comes over to the bed, squeezes my hand, and says, 'You were assaulted, attacked—'

'Who did it?' Mum makes a whimpering noise and wipes her cheek with her forearm. I crane my neck forward. 'Who, I said?' There is a shooting pain in my head. 'Ahh!'

'Be careful darling, you're injured. Relax, don't worry about it for now.'

'Who fucking did it?'

She inhales sharply through her nose. *Just spit it out.* She says, 'Don't know. The police are looking for them.'

'Was I mugged?'

'No! Your phone wasn't stolen.' *In that case it was either some random weirdo, Dunce, or Rat.* 'The police think it was some sort of personal vendetta.' *Rat or Dunce.* She squeezes my hand. 'Who would do something like this? You haven't been having issues with anyone, have you?' *I don't think Dunce knows where I live. And how would he know I was walking home from the bus stop.* 'Horatio.'

'No, I haven't had any issues with anyone.'

'That's what I thought.' Mum raises her chin and mutters, 'If it's not personal, then there's some lunatic out there.' She shudders and lowers her chin. 'Some sort of sicko, maybe a serial killer.' *Serial killers aren't sickos, Mum! Some are – Jeffrey Dahmer, Fred West. But lots of them aren't, such as my father, and me. Well, soon enough.* Her phone is ringing. She strokes my arm. 'Don't worry, they'll catch whoever did it. I'm sure they will. Try and get some rest.' She takes her phone from her handbag and answers it. 'Hello ... One second.'

She leaves the room and closes the door. Chances of someone randomly attacking me must be pretty slim. I close my eyes. The thudding in my head is decreasing. Could've been Dunce. But I'm thinking Rat. How dare whoever it was do this to me? There's no way they're getting away with it, no way in hell. Will kill them slowly and take a memento. I'm woozy, these painkillers are kicking in already. Did they think they killed me? What happened exactly? So many questions. I yawn.

Been awake for nearly an hour. Feeling really dopey, a sort of super-stoned sensation. Doing complex algebra wouldn't be easy in this state. Good news is the headache is gone. Asked the doctor when I can go home. She said I need to stay in for observation for at least another night. When I woke up, Mum was sleeping in the chair in here. Said she *couldn't get a wink last night as was so worried*. No need to be now, seems I'm going to be fine, touch wood, fingers crossed. Mum got me some snacks, which I'm eating. Fortunately, she didn't get Lindt Lindor chocolate truffles, as I'm still a tad nauseous and not ready to handle them. I have a bite of Snickers. On the wheeled table beside the bed, my phone is vibrating. Mum brought me its charger. She's gone home and will return later. It's my sister.

'Hello.'

'How're you feeling?'

'Not great obviously, I'm in hospital. Painkillers are doing a fine job though.'

'Tried to phone you earlier but you were sleeping. Mum only told me what happened this morning because she didn't want me to be awake all night worrying. She said you could have suffered brain damage, even died. The signs so far though are you'll be alright. Minor skull fractures and some swelling to the brain. That's what she told me the doctor said. Must be a massive relief. Scary stuff!'

‘They haven’t told me all the details. But yeah, head injuries aren’t good.’

‘You could have died! Can’t believe somebody would do such a thing. It could’ve been a mad person who did it. Sort of thinking though, er, it might’ve been you know who.’ *Rat.* ‘Brandon’s friend, Rollie. Seems kind of unlikely he would do such a thing. Occurred to me though it could’ve been him, maybe. I mean we’re not a hundred percent sure, but we think he’s been hanging around by our house. And we know he’s pretty crazy. After all he got arrested at Brandon’s funeral. Remember?’

‘Ha ha, yeah.’ *Don’t make me laugh, it’s hurting my head.* ‘Ow!’

‘Are you okay?’

While rubbing my temples, I say, ‘Yeah.’

‘I didn’t say anything to Mum this morning when she phoned. She couldn’t talk for long as someone was trying to phone her. Otherwise, would’ve said something. We have to tell her I thought I saw Rollie. Was pretty sure it was him. She’ll go absolutely mental I didn’t tell her. Her sister had just died; I was trying to help … It sort of makes sense. Our tenant saw someone fitting his description. And there was the brick through the window. To me it didn’t seem random. Why would a stranger do it? And if it was Rollie I saw and the tenant saw, why would he be hanging around unless he was planning to do something … Mum told me he went totally crazy when Brandon died. Is he blaming us for his death in some way? As if we were supposed to be there to stop it or something. Makes no sense. But if he’s crazy, it might have been him who did it. Anyway, he’s the only person I can think of who could’ve done it. Can you think of anyone?’

‘No.’

‘Are you sure? This is important.’

‘Can’t think of anyone.’

‘Okay. We have to say something to Mum and the police need to know.’

‘Yeah.’

'Get well soon … Bye.'

I yawn. Great for pain these pills, but not good, ah, not, what's the word I'm looking for … conducive to doing anything else.

*

The following morning – I'm in bed, playing a game on my phone. The doctor told me I won't be going home today. She said I need to be observed for a while longer and this is standard procedure with head injuries. But there's nothing to worry about. In a few months, I should be back to *full fettle*. There is a phrase – every cloud has a silver lining. The silver lining is, I won't be returning to that hellhole pretending to be a school for a while. When I woke up today, I could remember a little of what happened. Can remember leaving the bus stop and walking towards home. Last thing I remember is passing a row of railings running along the side of small park not far from home. After that it's a blank.

There is a knock on the door. It's Mum and the usual doctor. The doctor asks me how I'm feeling. Then she leaves. Mum says, 'The police are coming to talk to us. They're on their way, will be here any minute now.' *Ah, what do I tell them?* 'Don't worry I'll be here with you.' She steps over to the bed. 'Make sure you tell them everything, however minor it might seem.'

I close my eyes. Don't think Dunce is organised enough to have pulled the attack off. He would have to have known I was on my way home. Plus, he needs his big brother to do anything. It's Rat most likely. Seems my sister hasn't mentioned him to Mum yet … There is a knock on the door. A nurse opens it, and a policeman and a policewoman step into the room. The policewoman says, 'How're you feeling?'

'Not too bad.'

She says, 'That's good.'

The policeman says, 'Yup.'

Mum says, 'Thanks for coming.'

They introduce themselves. The nurse brings two chairs in, and they sit down next to my Mum, facing my bed. The policewoman says they have some questions for me. Then she says, 'How does that sound?'

I shrug my shoulders. Mum says, 'Reply when you're asked something.'

The policewoman says, 'Horatio, we appreciate you've been through something very traumatic. And it could be painful for you being reminded of what happened.' *Just get on with it.* 'Do you remember being attacked?'

'No, don't remember anything.'

'Okay.' She writes on a notepad. 'What is the last thing you remember?'

'Walking past a row of railings running along the side of the small park near my house.'

'Clifton Green?'

'Yeah, Clifton Green.'

Now the policeman is writing on a notepad. The policewoman says, 'Do you have any recollection of anyone following you?'

'No, none.'

She asks, 'Do you remember there being many people around?'

'When I got off the bus it was very busy. There were loads of people on the street. But in the side streets it was quiet. Remember seeing a Deliveroo scooter and a jogger. The jogger was wearing fluorescent pink.'

The policeman asks, 'Any idea who might have attacked you?' I shake my head. *Not mentioning Rat or Dunce. Will deal with them myself. I'm no rat.* 'Is there anyone who might have a vendetta against you? Who might want to hurt you for whatever reason?'

'No.'

'Even if it seems minor to you,' says the policewoman, 'we need to know if you've not been getting on with someone. It could be important.'

I shake my head again. *Ow*, hurts when I do that. Mum is peering up at the ceiling and nibbling on a fingernail. The policeman says, 'You were lucky. When the attack was unfolding, someone was leaving their house to put the rubbish out. They shouted at the attacker, and they ran off.'

'Otherwise,' says Mum. 'You could've, *hh*, died.'

That is one person I won't be killing. Not even if they have the best memento in the world. The policeman says the person who was putting out the rubbish gave them a few things to go on. They are also analysing CCTV from the area the attacker may have come from and fled in the direction of. And they are trying to get information from people who may have seen something. They claim there is a very good chance my attacker will be caught. They wish me a speedy recovery, say they'll be in touch, and stand up. Mum says, 'Can I have a quick word with you?'

She follows them out of the room.

EIGHT

I AM BEING PUMMELLED with a heavy object. The blows are raining down; blood is pouring from my head. I turtle up into a ball and scream for help. I awaken on my bed with my heart thumping in my chest. I sit up and wipe my sweaty face with a handkerchief. My head is throbbing. This is the second time I've had this nightmare. It is 15:23. Today is Wednesday. Returned home from hospital on Sunday afternoon. Not well enough to return to school yet, and that's no bad thing. On Monday will be though, so the doctor says. Not keen to. Would rather remain at home for a while longer, boring as it is here. I yawn. It is the meds which are making me tired all the time. It's why I keep dropping off in the daytime. Whoever put me through this is going to die, slowly. I clench the duvet. The throbbing in my head is getting stronger. I relax my grip and breathe in deeply through my nose. My bet is it was the coward, Rat.

I run my fingers over the bandages on my head. Got painkillers for the headaches. Not the badass ones though they gave me in the hospital. All in all though, haven't been feeling too bad considering what happened to me. Doctor seems to think the headaches will stop in a few days. I take the fly-fishing tin off my desk and empty the contents on the bed beside me. This is quite a collection. I put the crucifix necklace around my neck, the signet ring on the little finger of my left hand, and the monocle in my left eye. Then I haul myself off the bed, go into the bathroom, and look at my reflection in the mirror above the sink. Looking good. Well, would be if it wasn't for the bandages. I return to the bedroom, sit on the bed, and inspect the gold-capped tooth with the monocle. This might well be real gold and not fool's gold. And this is an incisor; Fool's Gold's was a molar. None the less it gets me thinking about my first kill.

I can picture Fool's Gold dead in the living room, as if it were yesterday. It is common for serial killers to revisit their kill sites. And that's what I'm going to do right now. Convenient location, what with it being in my house. Mum is at work. I take off the monocle, crucifix and signet ring, put everything in the fly-fishing tin, and go downstairs to the living room. To relive the kill properly, I need to move the furniture, so it is as it was the night I killed him.

The coffee table was in front of the television not in the far corner as it is now. I drag it over to the correct position. The sofa is by the far wall. It's supposed to be behind the coffee table facing the television. Doctor's orders were don't do anything strenuous for the next two weeks. But that sofa won't move itself. I lift one end and drag it across the floor. My phone is ringing. I lower the sofa then take the phone from the pocket of my tracksuit bottoms. Serena. I spoke to her a couple of times at the hospital.

'*Hi*, how're you feeling?'

'Not too bad.'

'Awesome. What're you up to?'

'I'm in the living room.'

'Doing what in the living room?'

'Moving some furniture.'

'*Hello*, you're meant to be resting, you've just come out of hospital.'

'Yeah, I know. But it has to be done.'

'You're crazy. Have they caught the psycho who did it yet?'

*

The following Monday – This will be the first class of my first day back. Can see through the glass pane in the door half the class are already here, including Dunce. *Ah!* My head is throbbing. I take a sharp inhalation of air through my mouth and enter the classroom. Tricia shrieks, 'Hurt your head Horatio! That's why you haven't been at school. Poor you.'

A boy says, 'Did your brain explode?'

'Nah,' says Dunce. 'He bashed it on the bottom of a bog. *Hihi.*'

Rahh! The throbbing is worse. Having dumped myself at a desk on the opposite side of the classroom to Dunce, I squeeze my eyes shut and inhale through my nose. The biology teacher comes in.

'Welcome back Horatio.' Can hear Dunce giggling. *Has to die! There is no other option.* 'The rate of photosynthesis is affected by three main factors: temperature, light intensity, and carbon dioxide concentration. A limiting factor is any factor that slows down the rate of photosynthesis if there is not enough of it …'

It's fairly unlikely Dunce attacked me. Makes no difference to him though, he's dead anyway for the bog flush. Was his fault it happened. But how will I kill him? Poisoning, pushing in front of a car?

All morning my classmates ask me what happened to my head. I tell them a driver knocked me off my bicycle. It's the quickest way. If I told them the truth, it would lead to more questions. Currently, I'm in McDonalds having lunch. Couldn't face the school canteen and yet more questions from pupils from other years. And quite possibly mocking too from those losers, the Daggerz. Fortunately, I have plenty of money thanks to the dealing I did out in Antigua. McDonalds isn't going to be too much of a hit on my finances. After polishing off my second cheeseburger, I start making my way back to school. Fair walk from here, and I don't want to walk too fast because of my injury.

Will be a bit late for my next class, French. My school sucks. It will surely come last or close to last in the school league tables. Deserves to, that's for sure. My phone beeps. It's a text from Mum.

Today, Now

Hi Darling, I'm picking you up from school at 2. Police want to see us at the 👮 station. School knows. 🤞Mum X

Have the police caught the person who attacked me? Quite possibly. Could be though they just want to ask me more questions. Mum was going to be picking me up from school anyway. Didn't want me travelling home alone she said, as I'm not a hundred percent. This means I've only got one more class left today.

Am about to turn the corner when I hear shouting coming from the direction of the school. What's going on? Youths in green tracksuits are flooding out from the basement exit. Having formed a semi-circle in front of the school, they chant, shout, and throw up gang signs at the pupils gathered on the steps. Positioned in the middle of them is the gang's boss, the lanky moron, Bad Dog. Best wait here for things to calm down. The main door bursts open and Darragh comes steaming through it.

'COME ON THEN YOU CUNTS!'

Daggerz are following behind him including Dunce. They throw themselves at their rivals. It's really kicking off. A C-Crew member has Dunce in a headlock and is punching him in the face. Excellent. Darragh grabs the boy punching his brother by his collar, pulls him off, and hurls him against a car bonnet. Shame that. Dunce is hurt though; he's bent over clutching his nose. I clap. Tricia and a girl from the rival gang are gripping each other's hair with one hand and punching their faces with the other. Dozens of pupils on the steps are filming the fight on their phones. The fight will be on *YouTube*.

A girl from the year above me is lying on the pavement being kicked in the side by Bad Dog. Darragh strides over to Bad Dog and puts him in a bearhug. He forces him to the ground, stands over him, and unleashes a punch. Bad Dog rolls over onto his front. Looks from here as if Darragh is securing a rear-naked choke. Teachers are racing onto the pavement. The female French teacher and the PE teacher grab onto Darragh's arms. If they hadn't come, Darragh would have choked that loser Bad Dog unconscious.

So much for Bad Dog's boasts in the flat; Darragh absolutely slaughtered him. The fighting is still going on. I move forward to get a closer look. There are boys and girls from both gangs lying bleeding on the pavement. Dunce is on all fours crawling up the steps. I rub my palms together. The C-Crew take off down the pavement. Well, the uninjured ones are. Others are limping, including Bad Dog. Renaming him Meagre Dog. *Ha!* I can hear a police siren. That's why they took off so quickly. A police car is speeding along the road after them. They are not the only police I will be seeing this afternoon.

Teachers are ushering the Daggerz gang inside. Two members of the gang are sitting on the pavement being attended to by teachers. One of them is Tricia's sister, the sixth former who stripped off my clothes in the toilets. I go inside. Darragh, Dunce and a dozen or so gang members are in the hallway. Dunce has a red-stained tissue held to his nose. He's not laughing now. Darragh smashes the wall with his fist and bellows, 'How fucking dare they!'

In the corridor outside a classroom, Tricia comes up to me, and says, 'Was a raid that, a smash 'n grab. C-Crew nicked all the hash. Three ounces, near on.'

*

Me and Mum are in the lobby of a police station. It is quite warm in here, so I take off my blazer, fold it in half, and place it on top of my mini rucksack. On the way here, Mum said she's *praying* they've caught whoever attacked me. The police haven't told her anything. There's a good chance they've caught him. Either that or they just want to ask me more questions. Maybe they've identified a suspect but haven't caught him yet. They might have some CCTV footage of someone they want me to look at, or run a description past me, and ask if I know who it might be.

Mum is nibbling her fingernails. I lean back in the plastic seat and tap my right index finger against my front teeth. Problem is if it's him, they are going to want to know everything. Don't want them finding out he attacked me at the bus stop, chased me with another man, threw a brick through the window, sprayed murderer on the wall outside my house. If they find out that happened, Mum and the police will know I'm hiding something. Best strategy, if it comes to it, is to keep shtum. Hurry up, what's keeping them? Don't want to be hanging around in here all afternoon. Though it's preferable to being at school. Mum is still nibbling her fingernails. Think I might use the algebra app on my phone. Beats staring at the wall. Here comes the policewoman from the hospital.

'Rakesha, Horatio, sorry for keeping you. This way please.' We follow her along a passageway. 'Horatio, how're you feeling?'

'Not too bad.'

'Good. That's really good.'

We go into a small room with white walls. There is a policeman sitting behind a desk. He is not the same one from the hospital. He tells us to sit down. Mum is still nibbling her fingernails. The policewoman sits on a chair to one side and a little behind the policeman. He introduces himself as a detective.

Then, after a pause, he says, 'I am the bearer of good news. We have a suspect in custody.'

Him? Mum blows air from her mouth, and says, 'That's what I was hoping for. Thank you so much; it's such a relief.' She lurches forward in her chair. 'Who is this suspect? Are you able to say?'

The detective swivels the computer screen on his desk, so it is facing us. On it there is some grainy CCTV footage of a man wearing a hood, standing on a pavement with a bag slung over his shoulder. He is tall, skinny, and has an exceptionally long nose. It's Rat alright.

'Oh my God!' Mum covers her mouth. She removes her hand and waves her hands in front of her face with the palms facing outwards. 'Grainy footage, and he's wearing a hood.' She stops waving her hands and leans forward. 'He's the spitting image of Rollie, the man I told your colleagues about at the hospital.' She swivels in her seat towards me. 'It's him, right? Rollie.'

'Yeah, could be.'

The detective says, 'Roland Barstow is currently in custody.'

Mum says, 'It is him.'

Yeah, that's what he said Mum. She puts her hand over her mouth again. The detective swivels the screen around.

'He hasn't confessed, but we're confident he's our man.'

Mum removes her hand, and says, 'Never truly believed he did it. Just thought I should mention his name, as he was the only person my daughter and I could think of. As I mentioned, one of my tenants saw a man fitting his description loitering near the house when it was rented out when we were away. My daughter also thought she saw him loitering near our house. W-why are you so sure it's Rollie who attacked my son?' She opens her arms. 'He had no reason to attack him.'

'He was in the vicinity,' says the detective, 'at exactly that time. The bag he's carrying in the footage is a tool bag. We believe he used a hammer from it to attack your son.' Mum gasps. *Makes sense. Cowardly Rat. How dare he do that to me?* 'Several witnesses have come forward to identify him. They told us he fits the description of a man they saw running from the direction of Godstowe Crescent.'

'Seems it was him then.' She shakes her head. 'Makes absolutely no sense though. W-why would Rollie attack, try and kill my son?'

She twists her head and looks at me. I shrug my shoulders. Her mouth is hanging open. The detective says, 'Can either of you think of any reason for Roland Barstow holding a vendetta against your family? Or you personally, Horatio?'

Mum says, 'Absolutely not.'

I say, 'No.'

'How could he attack my son?' She smacks her fists on her thighs. 'What did we ever do to him?' She pulls her hair. 'Makes no sense. He's obviously completely evil, mad, and probably on drugs.' She raises her chin. 'Oh my God!' She looks at the detective. 'He deserves to be locked up for a long time for this heinous crime.' Now she is looking at the policewoman. 'Against my defenceless son.' *Defenceless? I'm not defenceless. Cowardly Rat will be locked up for a long time, no doubt about it.* 'A-hh, Roland Barstow, Rollie as he's known, was out of his mind after the death of my partner.' *Fool's Gold.* 'You know my partner Brandon died, right?' *I should be getting the credit for that.* 'I mentioned it at the hospital.'

'Yes,' says the policewoman. 'I remember.'

Bet Mum didn't mention he died from an auto erotic asphyxiation accident. *Ha!* Mum says, 'Rollie was Brandon's friend, best friend.' She shakes her head rapidly several times. 'Don't know why Brandon wanted to be friends with that loser. I was never comfortable with him being in my house. He used to visit a fair bit.' Mum is looking at me. 'Didn't he?'

'Yeah, he did.'

'Think the only reason Brandon was friends with him was because he had known him since childhood. They went to school together. He was a bad influence on Brandon, I always thought. And this proves it.' She sighs. 'Rollie showed up at the house after Brandon's death. He was angry. By angry, I mean furious. Unhinged is how I'd describe him.' *Ha, remember it well.* Mum curls her fingers. 'A-hh, so don't want to revisit this. How dare that man do such a wicked thing.' She groans. 'Rollie was asking questions about Brandon's death. Then at the funeral, he kept approaching my son. Rollie was aggressively badgering Horatio. We, my sister and I that is, kept telling him to leave Horatio alone. But he wouldn't stop. Was like he had lost his mind. Straight after the funeral, at the cemetery, he was arrested by the police. For smoking weed, I think. We smelt it.'

Mum, he wasn't arrested for smoking weed, he was arrested because I phoned the police and told them he was trying to abuse children in the cemetery. I had put erotic asphyxiation materials, paraphernalia, in his bag. Sashes, pornographic pictures, Viagra. The police searched Rat and took him way. Screaming, he was.

'*Ha.*'

The detective is watching me. I bite the insides of my cheeks to stop myself laughing. Mum is covering her face with her hands. The detective puts his elbows on the desk, presses the fingertips of both hands together and stares at me. I look him in the eyes. He takes his elbows off the desk; Mum removes her hands from her face.

'Mr Barstow attacked you with a hammer from his tool bag. If a member of the public hadn't scared him off, you could have died.'

'H-hh, thank God,' says Mum. She grips my forearm. 'We'll forever be grateful to them.' She releases her grip and runs her fingernails across her thighs. 'He's going to pay for this. I want to see him locked up for a long time.'

Me too. Well, would prefer to kill Rat, but him being locked up in prison might have to do. The detective says, 'Roland Barstow has been charged with attempted murder. He'll have his day in court.'

'Good.' Mum sits up straight. 'A brick was thrown through our living room window. Wondering now if that was Rollie.'

It was him, Mum. In court, Rat could, most likely will, make accusations I ideally don't want Mum hearing. Even if they are … baseless, that's the word. She could also possibly find out some way or other I've seen Rat twice. And I didn't tell her. It would make me look bad.

'Why would that man attack and try to kill my son? Horatio never did anything to Rollie. We really appreciate you catching him. It gives us peace of mind. Right, darling?'

I nod and say 'Yes.'

*

The next day – I am in geography. Dunce is slouched at a desk three rows to my left. He has a plaster on the bridge of his nose and a fat lip. I chuckle. Tricia is slumped at the desk in front of him. Her right eye is swollen and there are scratch marks on her cheek. That was some fight. Yesterday, after the visit to the police station, I watched clips of the fight on *YouTube*. In one of them could clearly see Dunce getting a walloping. He is not a fighter like his big brother. Want to kill them both. I knock my fists into each other. The teacher is talking.

'Economic indicators include GNI. It stands for gross national income. Other indicators are the percentage of the population living below the poverty line …'

Dunce is chatting with the boy sitting next to him, who is a fellow gang member. They are probably plotting their revenge against the C-Crew. Not that it's up to them. It will be Darragh who decides what's going to happen. Tricia said their rivals stole near on three ounces of hash. Even if it's not high-end gear, must be worth at least seven hundred quid. Darragh will be angry and humiliated.

'Horatio!' That was the teacher. 'You're grinning. I take it you are enjoying my class.' *Sarcastic, this teacher is.* 'Can you give me an example of a social indicator?'

'Infant mortality rate.'

'Correct. Can anyone give me another?'

A few arms are raised. The teacher asks the boy with the crooked legs. He says, 'Life expectancy.'

'Yes. You lot are on fire today. Name another?'

Three pupils have their arms raised. One of the arms is Bart's. This is unusual, he never volunteers to answer questions. Teacher doesn't ask him though; he asks the Dinka.

'Literary rate.'

'Yes, Yeno.'

Assuming Darragh is going to want to get revenge, and he will, it means the Daggerz might well reciprocate in kind. Good word, reciprocate. *Hey Dunce, tell the class what reciprocate means? And then spell it? Rec-iprocate. Dance on TikTok, innit? No, moron. Now you die.* The Daggerz might launch a surprise attack on their rivals. Offsite, as in not at school. Possibly even at the C-Crew's base, the council estate, if they are planning to steal their stash. In the chaos, I could possibly kill Dunce, and maybe kill or at least hurt some of the others too. Need to find out what's being planned.

The mid-morning break has just begun, and I am on the ground floor near the stairs to the basement. Darragh, Dumper, Tricia's sister, and several other Daggerz are striding along the corridor towards me. I turn my back to them and bow my head. As they turn into the stairs, Darragh says, 'Patience is a virtue, Mustapha.' *Dumper!* 'Ever heard that?'

'Nah.'

I slink behind some pupils heading downstairs. On the stairs, I hear Tricia's sister say, 'Here's another. Revenge is a dish best served cold.'

Darragh says, 'Dig that.'

They are going to bide their time then. I don't want to be this close to them, but this is my chance to maybe find out what they've got planned. They are in the corridor now, and I am approximately six or seven metres behind them, at the back of the group of pupils I came down the stairs with.

'Here's a good 'un,' says Dumper. 'Revenge, the sweetest morsel to the mouth that ever was cooked in hell.'

'Looked that up on your phone,' says Tricia's sister.

'Trust you,' says Darragh, 'to pull one aht comparing revenge to grub. You fat bastard.'

Dumper says, 'Walter Scott said it.'

Tricia's sister says, 'Them teachers are wrong Mustapha, when they say you never learn anything.'

Darragh swivels around and bellows, 'Oi!' *Shit!* 'What you doing down here? Yeah you, Bog Diver.' *Rahh!* 'You might have bandages on your head 'n be in no fit state for diving in the khazis. But there's nothing stopping yah having a skinny dip in the urinals.' *Ah!* Everyone is laughing. 'Now fuck off!' I spin around and go back the way I came. 'Could sense he was here. Has a dark aura, the cunt!'

I slam my fists on the corridor's wall. My head is throbbing.

*

Seven hours later – I am in Serena's kitchen drinking Pepsi. Travelled here from school on the bus. Mum is going to drive me home. She doesn't want me being out late she said, after what happened. Which is ridiculous, as the police have caught Rat. Also, Mum is coming at seven-thirty which isn't late. I could have travelled home on the bus and been home long before it got dark. Tried to explain this to her, but she wasn't having any of it. Kept saying she didn't want me out on my own during the evening at the moment. *It's too soon.* Serena says, 'Drink up. Let's go and have a bong in the park.'

About to say I'd prefer a joint to a bong when her mother

walks into the kitchen, and says, 'Horatio, how's your recovery going?'

'Pretty good, fractures are healing quickly. The hospital thinks there's no lasting damage. Got one more scan next month, and then I'm in the clear.'

'Such a relief. Isn't it, sweety?'

'Ah *yeah*, for sure.'

'Spoke to your mother on the phone last week. She has it in for him, the man who did it to you. What a despicable thing to do to a boy.' She strokes her chin. 'Do you think he's mad, is that why he did it?'

I have a gulp of Pepsi, and reply, 'Quite possibly, yeah.'

'How could he do such a wicked thing if he wasn't?' *Because he thinks, knows, I killed his best friend. And there's the EA paraphernalia I put in his bag that got him sent to prison.* She touches my arm. 'Tell me if you don't want me discussing it. I appreciate you went through a really traumatic experience, no one, let alone someone your age should have to go through.'

'No, I don't mind.'

'So, the man who attacked you was a friend of your mother's partner. You knew him. He used to come round to the house your mother was saying—'

'Mum, enough already!'

We go to the living room. Serena is pushing the door shut when her mother calls out, 'Serena, leave it open.'

'Whatever.'

Serena leaves the door slightly ajar. I pass her five grammes of skunk for her and her school friends. She gives me five ten-pound notes. Through the partially open door, I see Serena's mother going upstairs. I make a joint out of my skunk. In the hallway, Serena shouts, 'Mum, we're going to the park!'

'Fine, but don't be too long. And remember Horatio isn't well.'

Serena scrunches up her face and says 'What does my mum think we're going to do in the park? Ollies on the skateboard ramp. *Hello.*' She swipes a strand of long, silky blonde hair off her face. 'Let's go.' We depart. Serena wraps her arm around mine. 'Crazy the stuff you get up to.'

'What do you mean?'

'Never met anyone before who has been attacked by a psycho with a hammer. And you've seen two dead bodies. Not just any dead bodies either. Your mum's boyfriend, and that rotting dude in Antigua. You've smoked crack too.' She kisses me on the cheek. 'What's happening with the psycho who attacked you?'

'Rat.'

'Yeah, Rat. There's going to be a trial, right? Your mother will get you a lawyer. And he will have a lawyer who will try and get him out of it.'

'He won't be getting out of it. The police know he attacked me and tried to kill me.'

'Try and get him the minimum sentence possible then. Would ask my dad to represent you, he's a lawyer. But he lives in Singapore. And anyway, he's a patent lawyer not a criminal lawyer.' We enter the park. 'Still can't believe Rat tried to kill you. Why would he do such a thing?'

'He doesn't like me.'

'No shit! Only thing I can think of, is he blames you for his best friend's death.'

'Yeah.'

'*Yeah.* Hello, he tried to kill you.' We pass the skateboard ramp. It's deserted. 'You were in the house when he died. Maybe Rat thinks you're responsible somehow.' She tugs my arm. 'Why're you smiling?'

'No reason.'

'There must be a reason; you don't smile for no reason.'

'Was thinking about Rat is all.'

'The dude who attacked you with a hammer makes you smile? You're weird.'

We smoke the joint in the usual spot, in the bushes in the

conservation area. Halfway through the joint Serena says, 'I'll be sixteen in a few months. Planning to have a combined party at my friend's house. Her birthday is three days after mine.' She passes me the joint. 'You're invited.' She strokes my arm. 'Bring a condom.'

'Excuse me.'

'You heard me, bring a condom. I don't want to be a slut, that's why I'm waiting until my sixteenth birthday to lose my virginity. You're a few months younger than me, so you'll be underage. *Hi*, which means I'll be a paedophile.' She passes her palm over my groin. 'But I'm guessing that won't be a problem.'

'You guessed right.'

'Thought so.' She nibbles on my ear. I pass her the joint. 'You better wait until then.' She exhales a plume of smoke. 'Don't fuck any sluts at your school. Or else!' *Serena doesn't know I'm not a virgin.* 'Promise.'

'Yeah.'

'Say I promise.'

'I promise.'

If there is going to be a fight between the gangs, I could turn up with my face covered, and in the chaos stab Dunce to death, grab a memento, and escape. Might even get a chance to stab some of the others. It would be blamed on the rival gang, not me. Because I am not a member of the Daggerz, no one will suspect I was even there. I need to find out what's being planned.

*

Two days later – It is the last class of the day. Tricia is slouched at a desk two rows in front of me, fiddling with her phone under the desk. Tricia is the only gang member who might tell me what is being planned. When the class ends, I follow her along the corridors. She is with her sister and another girl from the gang. Darragh, Dumper and some other gang members are in the hallway. Darragh says, 'Oi, oi!'

He drapes one arm over Tricia's sister's shoulders and his other over Tricia's shoulders. I slip through the hallway, go outside, and cross the road. Several minutes have passed when the gang members leave the building. Dunce is with them, as is Bart. He is not a member of the gang. Why is he with them? A female gang member clambers into a car. The others turn left towards the bus stop. Except Tricia who goes right. I cross the road and follow her. Walked about twenty metres when she spins around.

'Horatio, you following me?'

'No.'

'You don't normally walk this way.'

'I am today. Going to the train station.'

'Walk with me then.'

'Okay.'

'Didn't want to go with the rest of them. They're going to get stoned. They do the same thing virtually every day. Gets boring after a while. When are the bandages coming off?'

'Soon.'

'That's good.' She laces her arm over mine. *Don't touch me!* 'Have they caught the drunk or drugged-up driver who drove into you yet?'

'Not yet, no.'

'Who came up with your name?'

'My father.'

'Old fashioned name. Never come across a Horatio before you. Guess after the Battle of Trafalgar, baby boys were being named Horatio left, right and centre.' *Tricia knows about the Battle of Trafalgar. That's a surprise.* 'Bit like half the boys today being named Kai.'

'Kai?'

'The winner of *Love Island* Series Nine.' *Hate that programme.* 'You're pulling a face? Take it you don't like *Love Island*?'

'Hate it.'

'Hate is a bit strong, innit?' She wipes strands of greasy looking dirty blonde hair off her forehead. 'You might have romance issues.' She twists her head towards me. 'I could help you with them.'

Eeew! Right, let's get to the point. I ask, 'Are the gang going to be after revenge for the C-Crew starting the riot outside school?'

'Well *yeah*. No fucking way Darragh would let them get away with it.'

'What has Darragh got planned for them?'

Tricia spits a lump of chewing gum in a bin, grabs my ears and forces her tongue into my mouth. *Yuck!* Can't resist though, as I need information. I put my tongue in her mouth. I pull my mouth off her, and ask, 'Will it be a revenge attack?'

'You do have romance issues.' We keep walking. 'You're not an informer for the C-Crew, are yah?'

'No, of course not.'

'Good. Cos if you were, you'd get worse than a bog flush.' *Ah!* 'They'd probably crucify you. Similar to the army a gang is. In the army, if there's an offensive coming up, the top general, field marshal, or whoever will only discuss the details with his top commanders. Only last minute will he tell the army. Otherwise, the cat would be out the bag. Word would get about and it wouldn't be a secret anymore. Same with our gang. We know something big is coming up, on a weekend most likely is what're we're hearing. Will be a surprise, as they associate us with school. They think of us as a Monday to Friday thing cos that's when we're in their area, hood, whatever you want to call this shithole. Something will probably be posted last minute on our *Facebook* page. That's what normally happens.'

NINE

FRIDAY – TWO WEEKS LATER – The bandages were taken off on Wednesday. Had a scan too. I just got the results. They are good; I am recovering fast. Still get a throbbing in my head sometimes, and I am not meant to do strenuous exercise. The doctor strongly recommended I don't return to the boxing gym for another two months, which is annoying. How dare Rat disrupt my life? I bend my knees and throw a right cross to his body followed by a left jab to the tip of his beak-like nose. He staggers back, I shuffle forward and hit him with a right hook to the side of his head which drops him to the floor. I stomp on him. Rat isn't going to be my next kill, even though he deserves to be after the cowardly attack with the hammer. He wasn't prepared to face me toe-to-toe after what happened at the bus stop that time. Rat knew I'd get the better of him even though he is an adult, and I am a teenager. I would have embarrassed him.

Yesterday after school, I went to a law firm with Mum and met the lawyer who will be representing me. She sounded confident Rat would be getting the maximum term for his *wicked attack*. The lawyer thinks the trial is a way off. She didn't give a specific timeframe but did say she is working hard on my case. Will be meeting with her when a date has been set for the trial. Wish I could kill Rat, take a memento off him, and be done with it. Rat isn't the sort to own anything that would make a cool memento.

However, could always take the one remarkable thing about him. His nose. Would need to get it preserved of course. What's the name for the people who preserve animals …? I click my fingers. Taxidermists, that's it. Would keep the nose in a jar of vinegar on my bookshelf. Serena would come into my room, point at it, and ask, *What's that gross thing on the bookshelf?* I'd say, *A jarred curiosity.* The Victorians were into jarred curiosities. Specimens, foetuses, and body parts pickled in jars.

I switch on the iPad and go to *Facebook* for the third time since returning from school two hours ago. There is still no update on the Daggerz's page about the forthcoming fight, ambush, or whatever they are supposedly planning. I slam my fist on the desk. Why is nothing happening? Maybe Tricia was wrong, and they won't post anything on *Facebook.* Darragh or whoever will just text everyone when the time comes. If it comes. I slam my fist on the desk.

The *Facebook* page has had no updates in over two weeks. There isn't much on the page other than some photographs and comments. In one photo, the gang are posing and making their gang sign – the little finger of the right hand held horizontally at the bottom of the left index finger. There are also pictures of their logo – a red circle with a knife in the middle and *DAGGERZ* sprayed below it. There are photos of their logo on the wall outside school and on the wall surrounding the council estate, the C-Crew's headquarters. Come on, update! This could be my only chance to get revenge for a very long time. I close my eyes. In my mind, I see myself being lowered into the filthy toilet.

'Ahh!'

I leap off the chair, grab a pillow from the bed and slam it on the floor. My head is throbbing. I rub my eyes with the balls of my palms and take deep breaths through my mouth. Mum is calling me. I go downstairs. She is in the kitchen, stirring pasta sauce on the hob with a wooden spoon. Dinner isn't even ready yet. Why is she calling me?

'The scan was a relief.'

'Yeah.'

'Yeah! Is that all you have to say?' She stops stirring, twists her head and glares at me. 'You have to be appreciative. Look what happened to Tanice.' *What's that got to do with it?* She is still glaring at me. 'Health isn't something one can take for granted.' The sauce is bubbling. 'Do you understand what I'm saying?'

'Mum, the sauce is burning.'

She sighs, swivels and stirs the sauce. It's tomato, pancetta and olives. Should be pretty good. Mum hasn't got many good recipes; this is one of them. You can't go too wrong with pasta.

'The person who came out of their house and confronted that animal saved your life, or saved you from being brain damaged and spending the rest of your life in a wheelchair. Bloody maniac!' Mum slams her palm on a counter. The wooden spoon leaps up in the air, spins and lands on the floor. 'AHH!'

'Mum.'

She bends down, picks up the spoon, runs it under the cold tap in the sink, and says, 'Sorry, was so angry for a moment there. I could kill that man.' *You and me both.* She resumes stirring the sauce. 'What I still don't get, is why he did it. Been thinking about it loads, and it makes no sense at all. Must've gone mad, was on drugs probably, and thinks we're somehow to blame for what happened to Brandon.' Mum said exactly the same thing when we went to see the lawyer. 'At the trial, he might say why he did it.'

*

13:15 – The next day – Just got back from the shops. I push open the front door, drop the bag I'm carrying on the floor and run upstairs. Mum calls after me, 'Slow down, you're not a hundred percent yet.'

The iPad is on my desk. I enter its password, connect to the internet, type *Facebook* into the browser and … Still nothing! No update. I scratch the surface of the desk. Can't keep checking the iPad every two seconds, every weekend, forever. I'm not viewing the *Facebook* page from my phone, in case something happens and it is checked by the police. They might wonder why I was visiting that page as I'm not part of the gang. It's much less likely they would check my mum's iPad. Will be deleting the history anyway. What's with the delay? Is anything even going to happen? Or has it already and I missed it. I kick the wall.

'Horatio!' *Leave me alone.* 'Come down and help put away the shopping.'

In the kitchen, I unload vegetables from a shopping bag into the fridge's salad tray. When we were out shopping, Mum went to a clothes shop. While she was in there, I checked out the mall. There was a kitchenware shop in there. They had an impressive collection of knives. Steak knives, filleting knives, cheese knives, bread knives, boning knives, butcher's knives, grapefruit knives, cleavers. Hacking Dunce, Darragh, Dumper or Rat apart with a cleaver would be a lot of fun. Hacking them all apart with a cleaver, even more so.

'You've stopped. You're standing there like a statue. Put the stuff in this bag away.' Mum is gripping the handle of a plastic bag on the kitchen table. 'This is stuff for the cupboards.' I take two tins of tomatoes from the bag and put them in a cupboard. A filleting knife would do the job. It would be easy to conceal. Could whip it out and stick it between ribs into the heart. Or otherwise plunge it into the liver. I pretend I am holding a filleting knife in my right hand. Angle it slightly upwards and thrust. 'What're you doing that for?' I take rice and pasta from the bag and put them in the same cupboard as the tins of tomatoes. Mum takes the empty bags and stuffs them in a cupboard. 'All done. I've got some paperwork to do for Tanice's flat. What're you going to do now?'

'Might watch television.'

'Okay, see you in a bit.'

Already had lunch, we went to KFC. I watch some television in the living room. Then I turn it off and remember how it was in here when I killed Fool's Gold. Can't move the furniture to where it was that night, as Mum is in the house. I go into the garden and do shadow boxing. Jab, right cross, left hook, right uppercut. I repeat the combination at a quicker speed, then do it at full speed. Mum calls out of her bedroom window, 'Stop it! You're not ready for exercise yet. Doctor's orders.'

'Mum, it's just shadow boxing.'

'Stop doing it!'

She closes the window. Can see from here the missing brick in the wall where the fly-fishing tin was concealed. It was quite something, finding that treasure trove. I go into the kitchen, fill a glass with water, head upstairs, and check *Facebook* on the iPad again. Still nothing. When I plunk the glass of water on the desk, some drops spill onto it. Having wiped them off with my sleeve, I open my email. There is an email from Dalilah, my girlfriend in Antigua. She says she misses me. After firing off a quick email to her, I study for a while. Then I check *Facebook* again. There is an update. It's a message. *Time 2 stir up the hornets' nest. Meet at base – 20:30.* Finally! I punch the air. This is the opportunity I've been waiting for. There is now the possibility I could go to school on Monday a serial killer. I press my palms together and squeeze my eyes shut. It has to work out; it will work out.

The Daggerz base is probably school, unless base is referring to somewhere else. The hornets' nest is surely the C-Crew's headquarters on the top floor of the council block. This is my chance. In the commotion I will stab Dunce. If I can't get to Dunce, will stab Darragh or Dumper. Probably Dumper, as he will offer less resistance than Darragh. Regardless, I'll have to get out of there pronto before the Daggerz realise what's happened, and the two gangs cotton on that I'm not a member of either of them. This is my chance though, and maybe my only chance for a long time. I have no idea how things will play out. But one way or another, I will find a way.

I need an excuse to be out of the house. Serena doesn't live far away from the council estate – three or four stops on the bus. She better not be doing anything this evening. If Serena is, she'll have to cancel her plans. I phone her.

'*Hi*. What's up?'

'What're you up to later?'

'Going shopping with my mum.'

'What time will you be done?'

'Five-thirty ish.'

'Can I come round after that?'

'Sure. Six?'

'Yeah. Bye.'

'Why're you in such a ru—'

I hang up. Can hear Mum and my sister talking in the hallway. My sister must have just arrived. She's back from college, again. I go downstairs. They are leaning against the wall facing each other. The hall and kitchen are the new living room for them. My sister says, 'Hi Horatio?'

'Hello.'

'Your bandages are off.'

'Yeah.'

'Doesn't mean he's fully recovered though.' Mum swivels towards me. 'You have to take it easy for now.'

About to tell Mum I am going to Serena's later when my sister says, 'We're talking about the summer holidays.'

Mum says, 'As I'm going to be getting rent from Tanice's flat, we're going to have more money. We should go somewhere.'

'Mum's thinking Italy.'

Mum says, 'I want to visit Tuscany. Florence and Siena particularly.'

'Would love to go to Rome,' says my sister. 'And see the Coliseum, Trevi Fountain, St. Peter's Basilica …' *Leave Serena's, go to the estate, wait for the gang to arrive, put on a disguise, and during the fight stab Dunce, run off, take off the disguise, get on the bus, go home. It'll be blamed on the C-Crew. Will be as if I was never there.* 'If we're in Italy Mum, we have to see The Leaning Tower of Pisa—'

'Mum!'

'What?'

'I'm going to Serena's later.'

'I'll need to speak to her mother.'

'Fine.'

'We're going to the flat,' says my sister. 'Meeting a decorator there to discuss stuff that needs doing before it can be rented out. Want to come?'

'No.'

'No thank you,' says Mum. 'Right, let's get going.'

They depart; I go upstairs. In the bottom drawer of the chest of drawers, there is a black woolly hat I've only worn a couple of times. Could cut holes in it and wear it as a balaclava. In the drawer above are black tracksuit bottoms I don't wear anymore, as they are a bit small for me. If I get blood on them, can just bin them. Same with this brown long sleeve top I never wear. Will take rubber kitchen gloves from the kitchen, so I don't leave fingerprints. As for a murder weapon, it's got to be a knife really. Shot my last kill, my second kill, the drug dealer in Antigua with his own gun. But I can't get hold of a gun. I wouldn't use a hammer, as it is the weapon the coward Rat used. Besides, a hammer wouldn't be fast enough. I need to be in and out of there. Knives are what gangs in London tend to use. And I am pretending to be a gang member.

I race downstairs to the kitchen and pull open the drawer with the knives in it. It's a meagre selection. Could do with one of those knives from the kitchenware shop in the mall. There are two kitchen knives, which are both blunt. This steak knife has seen better days and it's blunt. I take out a small knife and hold it up. It's a paring knife. Would struggle to kill a mouse with this.

There is a filleting knife in here though. It has a wooden

handle that's easy to grip. Problem is it's also blunt. There is a knife sharpener in the drawer. I run the blade back and forth across it. I touch the tip of the knife. It's sharp, but not sharp enough. I continue sharpening … Perfect. It'll slide straight in. I practice thrusting it through the air, picturing the point penetrating between the ribs into the heart. Otherwise, it'll be under the ribcage into the liver like this. Or, if he is wearing too many clothes, the point will be driven straight through the throat. Three options there.

I take the knife, go up to my room and cut holes with scissors in the woolly hat for my eyes and mouth. The balaclava, tracksuit bottoms, long-sleeve top, kitchen gloves, knife, and a pinch of skunk wrapped in a tissue are put in a plastic bag. The plastic bag is stashed outside the front of the house behind the bins because I don't want Mum seeing me with it and asking what's in it. Back in my room, I reach under the chest of drawers and remove the fly-fishing tin. I sit on the bed and pour the contents on the duvet. Wonder how my father felt before killing people. Excited, I bet. But focused too.

Will I kill anyone though? The plan isn't precise. Depends on a whole load of factors outside of my control. My head is throbbing. After rubbing my temples with my knuckles, I pick up the crucifix necklace, hold it up, and watch the light reflecting off it. The throbbing diminishes. I am feeling calm. They're back, can hear them talking downstairs. I stay in my room until it's nearly time to leave. Then I go downstairs. Mum is in the kitchen. When I walk in, she says, 'Spoke to Serena's mother and she's fine with you going there. Thing is a friend has just asked me to go for a drink. Picking you up could be an issue as it's a little way away. I'll ask Shaneeka to collect you.'

'Mum, I don't need to be collected! I can come home on my own.'

'Are you sure you're happy to?'

'Yes, Ra-Rollie was arrested. It's safe.'

She blows air from her mouth, and says, 'It's too soon. And besides you're still young.'

'I was fine doing it before.'

She looks up at the ceiling and murmurs something. Then she looks at me and says, 'Okay, but be home by nine-fifteen.'

Will be later than that. They're not meeting at base until eight-thirty. 'Mum, it's a Saturday. There's no school tomorrow. Make it ten.'

'No! I want you home before dark.'

'Will still be light at nine-fifteen Mum, it's summer. Doesn't get dark for at least another half an hour.'

'Nine-fifteen. Take it or leave it.'

Ah, no point arguing. 'Fine.'

'Okay.' She wags her right index finger at me. 'Don't be late!'

'I won't.'

'And answer your phone if I ring. Have a good time.'

'Bye.'

I leave the house, pick up the plastic bag from behind the bins, and go through the front gate. Knife crime is a gang-related problem. I am not a gang member and I am a star pupil, so no one would suspect me of stabbing anyone. Will wait until the fight is in full frenzy then race in, stab, and run off before anyone has realised what's happened. Needs to play out like that. It has to. There is no other option.

Assuming school is base, it's only a short walk to the estate. Meeting at eight-thirty means theoretically they could be at the estate by eight-forty, eight-fifty. With any luck it kicks off straight away outside the block. Just have to stab Dunce and hopefully one or two more then get the bus home. Might be twenty minutes late, not the end of the world. I will blame it on the bus. It was that street on the left where I was attacked. *Rat!* It's drizzling. I pull up the collar of my polo shirt. This will work out. When I return to school on Monday, I will be a serial killer, and the gang will have lost a member. Ideally Dunce. My class will be infinitely better without the idiot in it. Bog flushing me was a big mistake.

I ring the doorbell. Serena's mother opens the door and says, 'Come on in.' I go into the hallway. 'Serena is getting ready; she won't be a minute. I'll get you a drink.' There is a woman in the kitchen drinking wine. 'Horatio, this is my friend Izzy.'

'Hi Horatio.'

'Hello.'

'You're cute. Can see why Serena likes you so much.'

Serena's mother slaps her on the arm, and says, 'Horatio, Pepsi?'

'Yes please.'

'You have an incredible name. Is your father in the navy, is that why you're called Horatio?'

'No, he's dead.'

'Oh!'

Think she's drunk. Serena's mother says, 'How's your recovery going?'

'Good. Head throbs a bit but otherwise I'm fine.'

'Oh my God! You're the kid who was attacked by the mad man with the hammer.'

'Yeah, that's me.'

Serena's mother passes me a can of Pepsi, and says, 'Poor boy.'

'Why did he do it? Attack you I mean.'

I shrug my shoulders and say, 'Don't know.'

Can hear running footsteps on the stairs. Serena skips into the kitchen and brushes a length of long, blonde silky hair off her face.

'Hey, what's up?'

'Just starting on a Pepsi.'

Serena is wearing a pink mini skirt, matching sleeveless top, white ankle length socks and white trainers. The women are staring at her. Serena's mother has raised her eyebrows. Her friend says, 'Wow!'

'*What*?' Serena tugs on my forearm. 'Come to the living room.'

Her mother calls after us, 'Serena, leave the door open.'

'Whatever.'

Serena dumps herself on the sofa. I sit next to her. She weaves her arm around mine and says in a quiet voice, 'Why were they staring at me? So rude of them.' She sighs. 'Izzy's a drunken slut. She's such a bad influence on my mum. Not letting her anywhere near you.' Serena kisses me on the cheek and rubs the inside of my thigh. I check the time on my Swatch. 18:09. 'Why're you checking the time?'

'No reason.'

They are meeting at base in two hours and twenty-one minutes. Will it be outside school? Is that what 'base' meant in the message? Serena whispers in my ear, 'Are you stoned? You seem spaced out and distracted.' She drags the fingers of her right hand across her top. 'You like?'

I raise my left thumb. After playing *Gran Turismo*, we go to the park and smoke a joint. Serena's mother orders pizza for us. We watch *Thor*. It has Chris Hemsworth and Christian Bale in it. Bale plays Gorr the God Butcher. He is hellbent on vengeance against the gods and wants to kill them all. What an appropriate theme. I look at my Swatch. It's eight-ten. Time to get moving. I stand up.

'Where are you going?'

'Leaving.'

'*Hello*, the film isn't over yet.'

'Have something to do.'

'Oh,' she whispers, 'you're delivering skunk to someone.'

'Yeah.' Serena hugs my neck and kisses me on the mouth. I peer out of the living room door. Can see her mother and friend in the back garden. 'If your mother asks when I left, can you say I just left.'

'Sure thing. You don't want your mum finding out you went somewhere else after leaving here.'

In the front garden, I take off my polo shirt and jeans, and change into the long-sleeve top and tracksuit bottoms. Then I jog to the bus stop. The bus comes quite quickly. On the bus, I switch my phone off to be on the safe side. Locations of mobile phones can be tracked. I get off the bus and walk towards school, scanning the pavement ahead as I go. When I get to the street where my school is, I cross to the other side of the road, as don't want to be seen. There is no one outside the school. The time is 20:27. I wait by the corner. Have a good view of the school from here. They won't see me though … 20:29. I tap the toe of my right trainer on the pavement. Nothing is happening, no one has turned up.

Eight-thirty comes and goes. *Ah*, school is not what the message was referring to then. On the other side of the street, a woman is looking at me from a window. Been here too long. I wander off. They must be meeting somewhere else and are heading to the council estate from there. I walk in that direction … There are teenagers on the street. Some are smoking weed, can smell it from here. One is doing tricks on a skateboard.

Time to put the balaclava on. I pull it down to eye level. Not all the way, as wearing a balaclava here wouldn't be good. People might think I'm a hitman. Even worn as a hat though, it will make me less recognisable. Up ahead, is the low wall surrounding the estate with the C-Crew's graffiti on it. Can't see any Daggerz graffiti, or Daggerz. Don't want to draw attention to myself, so I walk slowly along the pavement then cross the road and walk back the way I came.

It's 20:43, and I am scanning the area in front of the council block. They still haven't appeared. Where the hell are they? Depending on where their base is, they could be ages. Maybe they're not planning to come for hours yet. Doubt their parents care if they're out late. Hurry up, this could be my only chance for ages. Months, years maybe. I can't go to school on Monday unless one of them is dead, preferably Dunce. On the other side of the road, a teenager on a skateboard is looking at me. Could be C-Crew. Better keep on the move, or they'll wonder what I'm doing here. I must get revenge; I must get my third kill. I turn around and walk off. Two teenage boys are strolling towards me. They may well be C-Crew members. Think I saw them at the fight outside school. I bow my head and keep walking. As they pass me, one of them murmurs something that sounds like *rent boy*. I feel the contours of the filleting knife in the plastic bag I'm holding.

20:47 – If they don't turn up soon, am going to have to abandon the mission and go home. This is turning into a disaster. I kick an empty Coca-Cola can into the road. Hurry up! Been on this street too long, I could draw attention. I go onto the grass in front of the council block with the plastic bag swinging beside me. A woman drinking from a beer can stumbles past. There is an exceedingly tall teenage boy loping along the pathway towards the block. It's Bart. He must be scoring skunk. Don't want him seeing me, so I bow my head and move away from the pathway. He's standing by the intercom next to the entrance. Now he is going inside.

It is 20:52. If something doesn't happen in the next five minutes, am going to have to go home. The boy on the skateboard is looking this way. In the open here, I could be spotted and challenged by the C-Crew. A woman wearing a hijab exits the block and drags a wheeled shopping bag along the pathway. I check the time on my Swatch. 20:54. Damn! Will wait one more minute. Bart has come out of the block and is standing in the entrance. Looks from here as if he's holding the door open. Can hear noise behind me. It sounds like running feet. I look over my shoulder. Charging along the pathway towards the block, is a gaggle of people wearing skull balaclavas. Must be a dozen of them. The one at the front is hefty. That'll be Darragh. Running behind him, is a stocky person wearing tracksuit bottoms with white Adidas stripes on them. Dunce. Finally, they're here. This is on. They come steaming past in a line. Some of them are making the Daggerz gang sign. There are thirteen of them.

So, this is why Bart is holding the door open. The Daggerz probably paid him to help them. They are flooding inside. Must be going to raid the headquarters on the top floor. I want the fight taking place outside, as I can easily run off. The door shuts and Bart comes loping along the pathway. I turn away from him. Haven't come this far to do nothing. Got to get in there. I pull the balaclava over my face, take the kitchen gloves from the bag, put them on, take out the filleting knife, insert it in the back pocket of my tracksuit bottoms with the blade sticking up, pull my top over it, and race over to the entrance. En route, I shove the plastic bag in my tracksuit bottoms' right pocket.

The entrance is closed. What do I do? Shouldn't really be hanging around out here in a balaclava. People will think I'm a hitman or a terrorist. Two small children and a woman pushing a pushchair are coming this way. I should move. The entrance door bursts open; I jump to the side. A girl with a phone clasped to her ear spills through it. I grab for the door, but it shuts. *No!*

'I don't know who they are, Mum. They're loads of them.' She is looking right at me. 'AHHHH!'

The door opens and two women bundle through it. I squirm past them, go inside, and press the down button for the lift. Above the lift are the numbers of the floors. The number fourteen is illuminated. Fourteen is one floor below the top floor. I jab the button again, but nothing happens. I keep jabbing it. Still nothing. The Daggerz may be blocking the lift, preventing the C-Crew from using it to escape. What's going on up there? Will have to take the stairs. I race into the stairwell.

A boy is hurtling down the stairs towards me. He stops and presses himself to the wall. I run past him and up to floor two … Keep going, I've got to get up there. Floor three. A fat woman lumbering down the stairs shrieks, turns around and lumbers up them. When I catch up with her, she crouches down and covers her face with her hands. I hurry past her. Floor four … Floor five … Floor six … My head is throbbing. I stop, take deep breaths through my nose, and continue onwards at a slower pace. What's going on up there? If there is a big fight taking place, I could stab Dunce then run off, as I originally planned.

Floor seven ... Floor eight ... Floor nine. Adults and children are gathered on floor ten's landing. When I charge through them, some of them gasp, a child screams, and a man grabs onto my top. I kick him, he releases his grip, and I keep running. Feeling quite out of breath and my head is throbbing. Can hear shouting and screaming from above. It's kicking off up there alright. Chaos, just what I need. Floor eleven ... Floor twelve ... Floor thirteen. The shouting and screaming are getting louder. Floor fourteen ... Only one more floor.

I lift the bottom of the balaclava up to allow air in. I am four steps away from the landing to floor fifteen when I hear, 'Get in your flat 'n close the fucking door.' *Darragh.* 'Yeah you, cunt!' A door slams shut. I ascend the last few steps, press myself to the wall and peer around the corner. The Daggerz gang are huddled together at the end of the corridor outside the flat where I bought the skunk. There are ten of them. The other three are probably manning the lift. 'PUSH!'

The C-Crew must be pushing the door from the other side. I'm thinking Bart left it on the latch. There is lots of shouting and swearing going on. Can see those white Adidas stripes. They're my target. Once it kicks off, I'll race in, stab him, and escape. The bigger Daggerz members, the sixth formers, are at the front pushing the door. There is going to be a massive fight when they get inside. This could be my opportunity. I reach behind me and touch the knife in my back pocket. They're still pushing. Behind me I hear footsteps. I swivel around. Two girls, aged eleven or twelve, are gaping up at me. They scamper off shrieking down the stairwell. *CRASH!* I swivel back around. Daggerz are steaming into the flat at the end of the corridor. It's on. I go into the corridor and edge along the wall towards the flat. There is commotion going on in there.

Six, no, seven Daggerz are still in the corridor. None of them have white stripes on their tracksuit bottoms. Dunce must be in the flat, as is Darragh. Would have to get past that lot to get inside. *Ah*, this isn't going to work! Need the fight to spread into the corridor. A woman's head is sticking out of the entrance to a flat on my right. She is looking straight at me. Her eyes open wide, her head retracts, the flat's door slams shut. I can hear banging behind me. A gaggle of youths pour from the stairwell into the corridor and come charging this way. More C-Crew members. Five of them – four teenage boys and a girl. I press myself against the wall. As they sprint past, one of the boys lashes out at me with his fist. I tilt to the side; the blow hits the wall. They pile into the Daggerz still in the corridor. There is punching, kicking, screaming and shouting going on. People are looking out from some of the flats.

Need to get this done. I slink into the stairwell and watch the fight unfold. A Daggerz gang member is thrown into the wall. He or she slides down it to the floor. The gang's flat's front door springs open and gang members spew into the corridor. It's mayhem. This is my opportunity. I edge further into the corridor. Between a tangle of legs, I catch a glimpse of three white stripes. I take the knife from the back pocket of my tracksuit bottoms, hold it under my top and continue edging forward.

It's carnage. They are punching, kicking, clawing, screaming, shouting. I can see the white stripes. Dunce is booting a rival gang member turtled up on the floor. I whip out the knife and keep moving forward. Dunce is approximately eight metres away. No one has noticed me. Following a single stab through the heart, I'll run down the stairwell and hide in a corridor until things calm down.

The C-Crew member Dunce was booting is scrambling on all fours along the corridor towards me. Blood is streaming from his nose. He clambers to his feet, lunges at me and grabs the front of my top. I bring my forehead crashing into his chin. He topples to his knees. I kick him in the groin. My head is throbbing. Several of the Daggerz skull masks are turned towards me. One of them is clapping. It's Dunce. He's meant to be dead, not congratulating me. This is a disaster. Someone is staggering out of the Daggerz's flat holding a baseball bat. It's the C-Crew's boss, Bad Dog. He is tripped over, the bat clatters on the floor. He clambers to his feet and takes off running.

'GET HIM!'

That was Darragh. Bad Dog sprints past me. Daggerz are chasing after him. Where's Dunce? There he is, near the rear with Darragh. If I stabbed him here, I wouldn't be able to escape. They rush past me, don't pay any attention to me, and continue running after Bad Dog. Bringing up the rear, is a wheezing fat person. Dumper. They are all steaming through a door at the far end of the corridor. The only people now in the corridor are four injured gang members sitting and lying on the floor. The door the gang steamed through is swinging open. I go through it. There is a flight of stairs going up to the roof. Can't see anyone on the roof, but I can hear them. I crouch behind an air vent.

'You lot!' Darragh. 'Clear off, split up, 'n man the stairwell 'n the entrance. Give us a head's up if there's trouble brewing.'

'Alright.'

That was Tricia's sister.

'See you in a bit.'

That was Tricia. There is the sound of trampling feet. Who is still up here? I put the plastic bag containing my clothes on the ground, edge around the vent, and peer out. Five Daggerz are standing in a line near the roof's edge with their backs to me. One of them has white Adidas stripes on their tracksuit bottoms. What do I do? I drop to a sitting position and tap the back of my head against the air vent. This isn't going to work. If I stab Dunce, I won't be able to escape. *Ah!* This is a disaster.

'Mustapha!' Darragh addressing Dumper. 'Block the exit in case Bad Dog does a runner.'

Can hear heavy footsteps on the other side of the air vent. I'm trapped up here. Everything is going wrong.

'Where you hiding?'

That was Dunce.

'Flush him aht.'

Darragh. I crawl around the air vent and peer out. They have split into pairs. Darragh and Dunce are walking clockwise across the roof, the other pair are going anti-clockwise. I could rush over and barge Dunce off the roof. But then I have nowhere to go. The other pair are going to see me if I stay here. Need to move. I go to the other side of the air vent. Dumper is directly behind me and has an unobstructed view of me from here. I keep crawling around the air vent. He hasn't seen me. A phone is ringing.

'Hello.' *Darragh …* 'Pigs are on their way. Let's move lads. Pronto.'

Fuck, I never got an opportunity. Will be waiting for ages for another one. I pull the balaclava up over my eyes. This is so unfair – 'Rahh!'

Will give them a minute or so to clear off. I walk over to the edge of the roof. Directly below is the entrance to the block. The Daggerz will be pouring out of it soon enough. Would love to drop boulders on them, or cauldrons of boiling tar like they did from on top of castle walls in medieval times. The police are on their way. It's time to leave. I pivot and step over to the exit. Can hear something behind me. When I spin around, I see Bad Dog dragging himself up by his arms onto the roof. He will be my third kill; the kill that makes me a serial killer. His chest and stomach are on the roof, and he is pushing up with his arms. It's too late to kick him off, will have to stab him. As I run over to him, I feel for the knife in the pocket of my tracksuit bottoms. But it's not there. Must've fallen out. Mission aborted. I swivel around.

'OI!'

Bad Dog grabs onto my top. I pivot and hit him with a short

right cross to the chin. He staggers backwards. I retract my right leg and kick him in the balls. He groans and bends forwards. His gold chain and medallion are hanging from his neck. The perfect memento. Bad Dog lifts his head and grimaces. I jab the tip of his nose; he throws an arcing punch with his right hand. It sails through the air and misses me. I kick him in the chest; he recoils to the edge of the roof. Bad Dog is teetering on the edge with his heels hanging off it and his arms held out horizontally at shoulder height at his sides. I reach forward with my left hand, grasp onto the gold chain, and pull. It breaks off; he jolts forward. I bend my knees and hit him with a right cross to his chest. He goes, 'MAHH!'

Bad Dog stumbles backwards and teeters on the edge of the roof again with his arms extended at his sides. Could flick him with my finger and he'd fall off. However, that's not the coup de grâce I'm looking for. I bend my knees, push upwards with my legs, and unleash a right uppercut to the underside of his chin. As if in slow motion, Bad Dog topples off the roof. I peer over the edge and watch him cartwheel through the air.

'*NO!*'

He smashes into the ground. I am officially a serial killer. There are loads of people surrounding him. They are the size of ants from up here. In the distance, I see multiple blue flashing lights. Darragh was right, the police are on their way. There is no time to celebrate, I need to get out of here. Don't want to be seen, so I pull the balaclava over my face, collect the plastic bag from by the air vent, shove my memento in it, run for the exit, and hurtle down the stairs.

A group of South Asians are on the thirteenth-floor landing. Indians, Bangladeshis maybe. One of them, a woman, stares up at me and squawks something in her language. None of them are budging. A man with his palms held out in front of him is blocking my route. When I collide with him, he somersaults backwards down the stairs … Floor twelve … Floor eleven … I continue running. My head is throbbing. No time to stop, just have to ignore it. I shoot past two old people chatting on a step.

On floor five's landing there is a group of teenagers. One trips me. I have a hand on the railing though so I don't fall over. I haul myself up, pick up the plastic bag which I dropped, and keep running. Lucky for that teenager I'm in a rush, or he'd be kill number four. Nearing floor three when I see a bulky person ahead of me descending the stairs. Can hear them wheezing from here. *Dumper*. I run up behind him and kick him with the ball of my right foot in the small of his back. He groans, tumbles down the steps, and lands with a bump on floor three's landing clutching his leg, and squealing through his ghost skull mask. Excellent, he's injured. My head is pounding. I slow to walking pace, clasp my hands behind my neck and breathe rapidly in and out through my mouth. Got to keep moving, the police are coming. Don't want to be walking out of the building with a balaclava on. However, I don't want my face being seen. The balaclava is the lesser of two evils.

The pounding has reduced to a throbbing. I jog down the remaining steps to the ground floor. What is going on out there? Have the police arrived? I grip onto the entrance's handle and take a deep inhalation through my nose. Behind me there is a creaking noise. When I look over my shoulder, I see the lift door opening. Five people are inside – a man, a woman, three children. The woman shrieks. Here goes. I pull the door open and step through it. People are huddled in a circle around the dead gang boss. Through the tangle of bodies, I see Bad Dog. His body looks normal other than a leg bent at an unnatural angle. But his head is mush. *Ha*, he must have dived headfirst into the concrete. No one is even looking at me.

I cut across the grass. Halfway across it when I hear wailing sirens. A police van is surging along the road ahead of me. I whip off the balaclava. The police van screeches around one hundred and eighty degrees and tears off in the opposite direction with its siren blaring. Must be in pursuit of the Daggerz. I stuff the balaclava in the plastic bag and trot to the road. It is nine-twenty. Mum won't be happy I'm late. No doubt she's sent me texts and left voicemails. Not switching on my phone till I'm near home though, as if anything happens, I don't want it to be traced to here. The police may well think Bad Dog fell off the roof when he was being chased or hiding up there. An ambulance is racing towards me. It's not an ambulance Dead Dog needs, it's a hearse.

The bus stop is directly ahead. But police motor bikes are blocking the road. A police car has pulled up at the side of the road and there are police on the pavement searching a group of youths. Can't see them clearly from here. One of them is big though. Reckon he is Darragh. And those are white stripes on one of their tracksuit bottoms. *Dunce!* He is supposed to be dead. I turn around and go back the way I came. There is a bin on my left, which I drop the balaclava and kitchen gloves into, as it wouldn't be good if the police searched me and found them. However, the police don't take any notice of me. I make my way along streets parallel to the main road then cut through onto the main road, walk to a bus stop, and wait there for a bus. A police van drives slowly past. It starts to get dark. My bus is here.

On the bus, I examine my trophy. On one side of the gold chain's medallion is an England flag, on the other a bulldog. Feels heavy and might well be made of real gold. But it's tacky, pikey. What sort of idiot would buy this and wear it as jewellery? Morons like the loser gang boss, Dead Dog.

'Ha, ha haha ...' Some of the passengers are staring at me. Makes for a great memento though. My father would be impressed. It was a satisfying experience, and a great way to be christened a serial killer, even if the C-Crew's boss was not the intended target. He must've been clinging from the roof the whole time to hide from Darragh and co. Nearly worked out for him until I hit him with that uppercut, he fell fifteen storeys, and his head was turned into mush. 'Ha, ha.'

Thinking about my kill so much I nearly miss my stop. When I get off the bus, I switch on my phone. There are eight missed calls, two voicemails, and three texts from Mum. Unbelievable. No point listening and reading them. I know she'll be mad I'm over an hour late. Need to think of an excuse ... Will just tell her I went for a walk in the park after leaving Serena's and fell asleep there.

Was hoping to slip into the house without Mum noticing. But the moment I step through the front door, she races out of the kitchen.

'Where have you been?' She grabs my forearm. 'Was worried sick.'

'I'm fine.'

'Where were you?'

'At Serena's—'

'I spoke to Serena's mother. She said you left there at eight-fifteen ish. Where did you go?'

'Went to the park near their house for a short walk because it was a nice evening. Was tired and fell asleep on a bench. That's why I'm—'

'Why didn't you answer my calls.'

'Because I was asleep. My phone was on silent.'

'Told you before you left.' She prods me in the chest. 'Answer your phone if I ring.'

'Well, I was asleep and didn't notice.'

'So why didn't you text or phone me when you woke up then, and realised you were going to be late?' I shrug my shoulders. 'Unbelievable! So worried I was. You're grounded.' She is pointing up. 'Go to your room.'

*

I awaken with something cold on my chest. It's my memento hanging from my neck like a medal, a gold medal. This will be my first full day as a serial killer. Was pretty intense in that council block. It wouldn't have worked out if I wasn't so opportunistic. Like that word, opportunistic. Kicking Dumper down the stairs was a lot of fun too. From the squeal, I think he hurt his leg quite badly. I cross my right index and middle fingers.

'Horatio!' That was Mum. Why's she calling me? I take my Swatch off the bedside table. Don't wear it in bed. Wouldn't normally wear a gold chain with a medallion in bed either. 08:47. Rarely wake up this late. I stretch my arms above my head. There is pounding on my bedroom door. 'Horatio!'

'What?'

'Don't what me!' I put the pillow over my face. 'Get up and come downstairs ... Did you hear me?'

'Yeah.'

Bossy Mum is this morning, like her sister Aunt Fatso and her stepmother Genevieve. Nightmare Genevieve is. I push the pillow off my face, get out of bed, pull on some tracksuit bottoms and a T-shirt, go to the bathroom, and then make my downstairs. Mum and my sister are sitting opposite each other at the kitchen table. I plunk myself on a chair at the head of the table and pour orange juice into a glass.

My sister murmurs, 'Good morning.' There is a plate in the middle of the table with toast on it. I take a piece. Could do with being hotter, but it will do. I spread butter on it then reach for the marmalade. They are both watching me. 'Was terrible what you put Mum through last night.' My sister is trouble too this morning. I open the jar of marmalade. 'It was incredibly selfish. Did you forget that the last time you went out during the evening, you were attacked and left for dead?' I spread marmalade on the toast. 'How could you not let Mum know where you were?'

Mum tuts, my sister sighs. I put my left hand in the pocket of my tracksuit bottoms and finger the gold chain. Mum says, 'Take your hand out of your pocket.' Bossy is the order of the day. I take my hand out of my pocket, pick up the toast and have a bite. Not bad this M&S marmalade. 'You're grounded.' *She said that last night.* 'This means no more visiting Serena in the evenings.' She is glaring at me. 'It's your fault for behaving so badly.' She is pointing at me. 'And if you think I believe you fell asleep in the park, you're mistaken.' *Whatever.* 'Nonsense if you ask me.' *No one is asking you.* 'You put me through hell last night. You don't care about anyone other than yourself.' I stand up. 'Where're you going?'

'To put more toast on.'

'You better not be this nonchalant when you face that man in court. Because it will not make a favourable impression.'

Mum storms out of the kitchen. My sister huffs, stands up, and says, 'Unbelievably selfish. How dare you frighten Mum. Do you have any idea how difficult it must've been for her letting you go out in the first place after what happened?'

She marches off. My sister is supposed to be at college, not here every weekend ... *Ping!* Toast is ready. I take the toast, sit down at the table, remove the gold chain from my pocket, and attach it to my neck. While eating the toast, I finger the gold medallion with the fingertips of my left hand. It is tacky and pikey, but it makes for a wonderful trophy, and a fabulous start to my collection. Kill number three; the kill that makes me a serial killer. Even if I end up killing as many people as the Doctor of Death, Harold Shipman, kill number three will always be special. This kill will be as memorable as my first kill. Can hear someone on the stairs. I slip the medallion under my T-shirt. Mum stomps into the kitchen.

'We're going to the supermarket. Won't be long, an hour tops. You are not to leave the house.' She is pointing at me. 'Is that understood? Answer me!'

'Yeah.'

'And clear up the table when you're done.'

Mum and my sister didn't bother clearing up anything. How selfish of them. The front door slams shut. After clearing up, I go into the living room, sit on the sofa, twirl the medallion in my fingertips, and remember last night. What an awesome uppercut it was. The best coup de grâce ever. I rearrange the furniture, so it is exactly as it was the night of my first kill. My phone is ringing. It's Serena.

'What the hell happened? Your mum was freaking out bigtime. She phoned and asked me when you left. I exaggerated and said you left a bit later than you did, like you said I should. She asked me if you had said anything to me about planning to go anywhere else after you left here. Frantic she was. Because you were attacked recently, I guess. Even my mum was nervous. I tried phoning you, but you didn't answer. Your mum phoned my mum at ten-thirty and said you'd showed up. *Well*, where were you?'

'Was delivering skunk to someone and got delayed. If I tell you something, promise me you won't tell anyone.'

'I promise.'

'I saw this idiot fall off a roof and die.'

'No way!'

'Yes way, I saw it. His head was mush.'

'Gross! And I don't believe you. There's no way you can keep seeing dead bodies the whole time, we're not living in a war zone. Your mum's boyfriend, the drug dealer in Antigua, and now this dude, in a really short space of time. How's it even possible? You're way more likely to win the lottery than for that to happen.'

'It's true, he fell off a roof.' I am rubbing the medallion with my thumb. 'His gang name was Bad Dog—'

'Got my record lap time on *Gran Turismo*. Absolutely killed it. So proud of myself right now ...'

I grit my teeth. How dare she interrupt me? After the call, I lie on the sofa, fiddle with the gold chain, and ponder what's going to happen. Didn't get to kill Dunce, and that's a real shame. However, the main reason I wanted to do it other than for revenge for the bog flush, was so I didn't have to go to school with the idiot anymore. And with any luck that could now happen. The police searched him, his brother, and some of the other gang members. They may well have found knives and drugs on them. Regardless, they could be in big trouble for being involved in the gang fight. The police will know they are Daggerz and there was beef between the gangs.

Even if they don't hold them responsible for Bad Dog's death, and think it was an accident, the police must think they contributed to it, by scaring him and chasing him onto the roof. People were injured in the fight too. Dunce, his brother and other Daggerz could be sent to a juvenile detention centre and be expelled from school. Them being expelled comes a poor second to killing them. But at least I'd never have to see Dunce or Darragh ever again. I press my palms together. *Please be expelled.* Right, best move the furniture before Mum returns from the supermarket.

TEN

THE NEXT DAY – I am in the first class of the day, geography. The good news is Dunce isn't here. I roll down the sleeve of my shirt and check the time. The class started twelve minutes ago. Even if he was late, he'd be here by now. I clench my fist. Tricia and the two boys from the gang are here though. I want to talk to Tricia and find out what is going on. Problem is she poled up when the class was starting, and I didn't get a chance to. However, she is sitting at the desk in front of me. Tricia is whispering to the girl at the desk on her right. I lean across my desk so I can hear what she is saying.

'I ran off. But Darragh, Dalton and some of the others got nabbed by the pigs. Three of ours ended up in hospital. Mustapha's still there.' I punch the air. 'My sister spoke to him. The fat bastard's leg is busted up bad.' *Excellent.* 'And that's not all. C-Crew's boss died.'

'No way!'

'Yes way.'

'You two,' says the teacher. 'Pipe down.'

They stop talking. I try to get Tricia's attention, but the teacher notices and tells me off. Will have to wait until the class ends. A good start to the day this though, what with Dunce being absent and Dumper in hospital. I undo the top button of my shirt and rub the gold medallion with my fingertips. When the class ends, I follow Tricia along the corridor. She is chatting with the two gang members from my class. I approach them.

'What's going on? Where's Dalton?'

'None of your beeswax,' says one of the boys.

The other says, 'Fuck off!'

'Tricia.'

'Don't worry your pretty little head about it; you'll find out soon enough.'

Something must have happened to him. If he was just pulling a sicky, she wouldn't have said that. I follow them into the classroom and listen to their conversation. Tricia says, 'Mustapha's leg is cunted.' *Know that. But what about Dunce and Darragh.* 'Bone was sticking out the side of his leg.'

'Bloody hell!' says one of the boys.

I snicker.

'The fat bastard,' says Tricia, 'is claiming he was pushed down the stairs.'

'Ha haha.'

'Horatio!' says Tricia. 'Stop laughing, it's not funny.'

One of the boys says, 'Mustapha's one of ours, don't be disrespectful.'

'He will get even fatter nah,' says the other boy. 'There's nothing to do in hospital but eat.'

The English teacher comes in and says, 'Stop talking please.'

She asks Tricia to read. Tricia stands up and reads in a posh voice – 'Five o'clock had hardly struck on the morning of the nineteenth of January, when Bessie brought a candle into my closet and found me already up and nearly dressed. I had risen half-an-hour before her entrance, and had washed my face, and put on my clothes by the light of a half-moon just setting, whose rays streamed through the narrow window near my crib …' The door opens. It's the headmaster. There is a policewoman behind him. Tricia murmurs, 'Shit.'

'Rahul, Ali, Tricia, come with us.'

The three gang members pick up their stuff and exit the classroom. They're in trouble too. The police either know or suspect they were at the fight. They don't know I was though. *Ha!* At lunchtime in the dining hall, I look for gang members. There aren't any. I ask some pupils from other years what's happened to them. They tell me the Daggerz either didn't show up at school today or were removed from class by the headmaster. Good news. However, it means I can't find out what's going on with Dunce and Darragh.

I'm in the last class of the day, chemistry. The teacher is explaining how endothermic reactions refer to chemical reactions which result in energy being transferred internally. Already know this. I am sitting in the back row, looking at my phone under the desk. Just received a text from Mum telling me to come straight home from school and not to dawdle. She wouldn't be any the wiser if I did dawdle; she won't be home from work till six-thirty.

I am searching online for updates on the gang fight. There are lots of social media posts on *Twitter*, *Instagram*, and *Facebook*. Some of them are from idiots claiming to be C-Crew members threatening revenge on the Daggerz. Several dozen messages on *Twitter* and *Instagram* have the hashtag RIP. They are for the dead gang boss whose medallion has popped out of the top of my shirt. Bad Dog. Now Dead Dog.

'Haha.'

'Horatio,' says the teacher. 'Something funny?'

*

Tuesday morning, at the start of the school day, is when assembly happens. Not every Tuesday though. Twice a month, usually. The whole school is crammed into the dining hall. The headmaster is standing in the middle with the teaching staff lined up beside him. I can see Tricia and the two other gang members from my class. So, the police let them go. Tricia's sister is here too. I waited in the corridor outside the dining hall until assembly started. Dunce and Darragh were a no-show. Is the headmaster going to give an update on what's going on with them? They have to be expelled; it is the school's duty. The headmaster is speaking.

'As many of you will be aware, a serious incident took place on Saturday evening. A gang-related riot at an apartment block, involving over a dozen pupils from our school. The participants, no, we'll call them transgressors.' *Doubt many of this lot know what transgressor means.* 'As they were hiding their faces behind masks, they no doubt thought they would get away with their disgusting behaviour.' His head moves from left to right. He is looking at gang members. 'However, they were sorely mistaken. All have now been identified, and the matter is being investigated by the police.' He wags his right index finger in the air. 'This incident resulted in multiple injuries to members of our school and the other party involved. Tragically, something even more serious occurred.' He pauses. 'This riot resulted in a death.'

There are gasps. A girl from the year below calls out, 'Headmaster, was it one of our lot?'

'Natalia, how dare you interrupt me during assembly!' I stick my right index finger between the buttons of my shirt and touch the gold medallion. 'The answer to your question is no. The details surrounding the young man's death are still being investigated. It is not known at this stage how he died, and who is responsible.' *Ha, and you'll never know.* 'There has been a lot of speculation on social media. I am asking you to refrain from partaking in this stupidity. It is utterly pointless and irresponsible. Horatio, stop grinning!' I lower the corners of my mouth to a horizontal position. 'There is nothing remotely amusing about this.' *You're wrong.* 'As I was saying, speculation online serves no purpose …

'A stern reminder to all of you. Gang-affiliated incidents slash behaviour will not be tolerated in our school. Going forward, anyone involved in any gang activity will be suspended. Anything that is proven to be serious, will result in expulsion …' *Say that has happened to Dunce and Darragh.* 'Those who were involved in Saturday's ruckus will regret participating in it, if they are not already.' *I won't be.* 'We will be writing to your parents and guardians to explain the situation.' *Not ideal. Mum might suspect I was there.* The headmaster is pointing at me. 'Yes, Horatio, that is a more suitable expression. Let's finish on a positive note. On Saturday, when some of you here were disgracing yourselves, over at the Barnet Copthall, at the Southern Area Finals, one of our own came first in the triple jump and long jump. Congratulations, Yeno.' The headmaster's left arm extends in the direction of the Dinka. 'A remarkable achievement. Let's all give a big round of applause for Yeno.'

There is clapping, and some booing too. Assembly is over. Everyone files out of the hall. A boy nudges me.

'What were you grinning for in there?'

'None of your business.'

'Go on.' He flicks my shoulder. 'Tell me.'

'Touch me again, I will punch you in the face.'

He tuts and moves away from me. If it's a letter the school are planning to send, I might be able to get rid of it before Mum sees it. She usually works from home two days a week. Hopefully the letter will arrive on a day she's at work. These cheapskates aren't going to fork out for hundreds of stamps. It'll be an email. Will just deny I was there. Tricia is chatting with a group of girls. Maybe they're discussing Dunce and Darragh. I weave through the pupils and get within earshot.

'Too many of us to expel, in't there?' says Tricia. 'Can't very well tell us all to fuck off. The headmaster is speaking shit. They don't know who did what. Not the pigs, and certainly not that arrogant twat. We were wearing masks. Headmaster can say you can't hide behind masks, but you can, to a certain extent anyway. That's what masks are for. Catch you lot later.'

Tricia turns right, the girls left. She joins the two male gang members from my class. When I approach them, the boys tell me to get lost. The school might not be able to expel all of them. However, they can surely expel the gang's boss Darragh and his horrible little brother. After all, Dunce is already in the school's bad books. And the gang fight, should, no, must, be the last straw.

I go into the classroom. All the desks near Tricia are taken, so I opt for one near the front. The maths teacher enters the classroom and says, 'Today we're going to be studying rates of change. A common rate of change is speed. Speed being the rate at which an object's distance changes in relation to the time taken …' *Child's play this.* 'Were we to plot a graph showing how the variables relate to each other, the rate of change is calculated by finding the gradient of the line.' The teacher draws a graph on the white-board. 'Does anyone know how to find the gradient?'

Can't be bothered to answer. The Bangladeshi girl raises her arm. I feel the outline of the chain under my shirt.

*

It's 18:33, and I've just heard the front door slam shut.

'HORATIO!' *Bollocks.* 'Get down here.' I put the pigtail in the fly-fishing tin, stuff the tin in my chest of drawers, exit my room, and go downstairs. Mum is standing in the hallway with her fists on her hips. 'Your school emailed me this morning.' *Ah!* 'There was a big gang fight involving lots of kids from your school at a council estate on Saturday evening. There were multiple injuries. And someone died! They fell to their death.' *No shit.* 'You're smiling.' She taps my cheek. 'Nothing funny about someone losing their life.' *You're wrong; there is.* 'The fight happened when you went AWOL.' She juts her chin at me. 'Where were you really after you left Serena's?'

'Told you already, fell asleep in the park.'

'Don't give me that. Who falls asleep in the park? I don't believe it for a second.' I shrug my shoulders. 'It's nonsense. Were you at the gang fight?'

'No.'

'Don't lie to me.' She prods my chest. 'I suspect you were there.'

'I wasn't. You don't even know what time it was on at. Might have taken place while I was at Serena's, or after I got home. Who knows?'

Following a huff, she says, 'You're grounded, and will be for a while.'

I go upstairs to my room. Haven't been in there long when Mum calls me. What now? Nightmare she's being. I go down to the kitchen. Mum tells me to lay the table. She then takes a knife from the knife drawer and rapidly cuts a red pepper into pieces. Must be having stir fry, again. She won't be needing the filleting knife in that case, which is fortunate as it's gone walkabout. Mum is now slicing a Chinese cabbage into strips. I put mats on the table and place forks on their left.

'We have a date for the court case. It's six weeks today.' *During my summer holiday.* 'The lawyer thought we'd be waiting a lot longer.' She pushes the vegetables with the knife into the wok and tosses the contents with a spatula.' *With any luck they'll give Rat the electric chair.* Mum throws a handful of shrimps into the wok. 'We'll be meeting with the lawyer week after next to start preparing for the trial.' Having tossed the contents of the wok about for approximately three minutes, she puts the food in the two bowls I have set on the counter. 'God knows what excuses that man is going to come up with in court.' She skewers a shrimp, puts it in her mouth, and chews on it. 'You're in the doghouse.'

*

The following day – The first class of the day, French, is starting in two minutes. The teacher hasn't arrived yet. I am sitting at a desk in the front row, looking directly ahead at the blank whiteboard and remembering obliterating soon-to-be Dead Dog with the uppercut which sent him toppling off the roof and plummeting to his death. Can feel his medallion hanging from my neck. It's a heavy piece of bling to be lugging around all day, every day. Not that I'm planning to. Will only be wearing it for a little while longer. Then I'll stuff it in the fly-fishing tin with the other mementos. There is a groan. That was the Bangladeshi girl in the row behind me. I twist my head. He is standing in the entrance to the classroom, swaying his hips from side to side. *No!*

'Miss me?'

He skips into the classroom. *Dunce, you are supposed to be dead. Or at least expelled.* He high-fives Tricia then rubs the top of the Bangladeshi girl's head.

'Don't touch me!'

He dumps himself at a desk and farts loudly – 'Hihi.'

Ahh, this can't be happening. School just got ten times worse. I grip the desk's legs and clench my teeth. The French teacher comes in, and says, *'Bonjour.'* I headbutt the desk. *'Horatio, quel est le problème?'*

I don't show up for the next class. Not bothered if the school tell Mum and she ends up grounding me for longer. I go outside and wander the streets. Why hasn't the useless school expelled him? It's not as if the gang fight is his first offence. Far from it. I stamp on an empty can of Fanta and kick it into the road. The only good news is the summer holidays are starting soon, and I won't have to see Dunce or his brother for seven weeks. Maybe Dunce is only back at school temporarily. If he's in trouble with the police, he could still be expelled. Wishful thinking probably. There might be a chance though. I need to find out what's going on. Having bunked the next class too, I return for the class before lunch. Maths.

I am sitting at a desk on the opposite side of the classroom to Dunce. The teacher is writing ratio questions on the whiteboard. Basic ones. *A sweet shop sells strawberry bonbons, lemon bonbons and chocolate bonbons. In one week, the number of strawberry bonbons sold, to lemon bonbons, to chocolate bonbons sold was in the ratio of 3:4:5. The total number of bonbons sold in the week was 728. Work out the number of strawberry bonbons sold?*

'What's a bonbon?'

Dunce!

'A bonbon,' says the teacher, 'is a chewy sweet with a thick layer of sugar dusting.'

'Dalton,' says Tricia, 'you never had a bonbon?'

'Nah.'

Tricia says, 'Yeno, bet you'd be hard pushed to find a bonbon in Darfur.'

Some of the pupils, including Dunce, are laughing. The idiot doesn't even know what Darfur is. The teacher says, 'Put up your hand if you know the answer.'

The Bangladeshi girl raises her arm. But the teacher asks me, even though I'm not volunteering. I work it out on my phone.

'One hundred and eighty-two.'

'Yeah, right answer.'

Tricia says, 'Got some competition in't yah, Banu?' The Bangladeshi girl. 'Smart you are, Horatio. Quick with numbers.'

The teacher says, 'Tricia, are you going to talk all the way through my class?'

'No, I'm done.'

'We'll continue then.'

A scrunched-up piece of paper lands on my desk. I look to the right. Dunce is punching his palm. *Ah!* Either I change school, or he dies. The bell goes and near on everyone races for the door.

I am in the dining hall, perched at the end of a table munching on an apple. The table two behind mine is full of sixth formers. Some of them are members of the gang. Darragh is there. Today just keeps getting worse. Want to know what's going on with him and his brother, so I shift over to the table next to them to eavesdrop. I continue eating the apple with my head bowed, so they won't notice me. Dunce, Tricia and two gang members from the year above me approach the table and squeeze onto the bench, on the other side of the table to Darragh. I keep my head down. Darragh says, 'Was telling this lot about Saturday. Mental it was. An absolute barn burner of a fight in that corridor. We gave them a good kicking … Pigs found nought on us.' I crush the apple core. Juice oozes between my fingers. 'We had got rid.'

Dunce says, 'Got shitloads of skunk.'

'A key,' says Tricia's sister.

Ah, that's worth a fortune. It keeps getting worse.

'As in a kilo?' says one of the sixth formers.

'*Yeah*,' says Tricia's sister. 'Not sure which was better, getting the gear or the wanker being reincarnated as tarmac.'

The whole table laughs. Tricia says, 'Some Saturday it was for jumping, what with Yeno in the triple and long jump, and Bad Dog in the high jump.'

They laugh louder. Darragh says, 'I'm renaming Bad Dog, Slush Puppy.'

They laugh even louder. I grit my teeth. It's me who should be taking the credit for this. Have his pikey medallion around my neck to prove it. Dunce says, 'When we were up on the roof, we never saw the cunt—'

'Oi!' says Darragh. 'What did I tell you?'

'Don't say nought cos it could be in-crim-in, ah.'

Moron. 'Precisely, incriminating. We did nought up there, if we were up there at all that is. We don't want anything being misconstrued. Goes for all of yah who were there.'

'Thing I don't get yeah,' says a male sixth form gang member. 'Who was the dude in the regular balaclava at the fight? Weirded me out he did.'

'Got stuck into their lot,' says Dunce. 'Was helping us aht.'

No, I was not! The apple core is mush. I wipe my palm on the table. Tricia's sister says, 'Not what Mustapha's saying. Been getting texts from him in the hospital. He's claiming the guardian angel in the balaclava pushed him down the stairs.'

'Bollocks!' says Darragh. 'Fat bastard doesn't want to admit he tripped over.' *I did it.* 'Wheezing, spluttering all over the shop he was. You'd think he was forty, not a teenager. What's the point of having all that weight if you can't throw it around. Good for nothing Mustapha is, other than for doing bad shits.' *Eeew!* They are laughing. 'Oi, Horatio.' *Ah!* 'You're so close to me, you could give me a rash. Move to another table.' *Die!* 'Nah! Or you'll be going for a swim in the khazi.'

Ffff, this is not how it was meant to be. I slide to the end of the bench and stand up. Dunce says, 'Yeah Horatio, piss off with your tail between your legs.'

I will torture you to death. Tricia says, 'Poor Horatio.'

Darragh says, 'Don't tell me you fancy bog brush.'

Ah! An apple core sails past my head. Bet Dunce threw it. On the way out of the dining room, I punch the wall.

*

Thursday – Two weeks later – The summer holidays started last Friday. My sister has gone to Greece with friends from her college. She is flushed with cash from Aunt Fatso and can go anywhere she wants. There is going to be no family holiday to Italy after all. Mum says it's because work is hectic and the trial is coming up. I'm not bothered. Would be a nightmare being in Italy with Mum and my sister. Want to go there on my own, or possibly with Serena. I am still grounded and have been stuck in the house most of the time. Went to the boxing gym on the weekend though. Did shadow boxing, pads and bags. I can't spar yet. Mum phoned the gym and told them. Might go to the evening class tomorrow, if Mum is free to pick me up.

The sun is shining through the bedroom window onto my mementos, which are laid out in front of me on the desk. I grip the gold chain and swing the medallion back and forth like a pendulum. While swinging it, I remember the epic uppercut I hit

Bad Dog with that sent him toppling to his death. Not in the entire history of uppercuts, can there have been one as sensational. It deserved to be televised to a live audience.

I don't want to return to that school. Mum says I'm stuck there, at least until I do my GCSE's next summer. It's far too long to wait. Darragh's got one more year, and Dunce is going to be there. Will be intolerable. Can't do it; I won't do it. I stand up, move to the middle of the floor, bend my knees, retract my right arm at my side, push up with my legs, and deliver an uppercut to the underside of Dunce's chin. It lifts him up off the ground. The word *Bang!* appears in a red zigzagged circle, like in old comics when the superhero hits the baddies. Dunce is quivering on the floor. I step forward, bend over him and unleash ground and pound until his head is mush, same as Bad Dog's was after hitting the concrete from fifteen storeys up. Feeling out of breath and my head is throbbing. I clasp my hands behind my neck and get my breath back.

The floorboards are creaking on the landing outside my room. I hurry over to the desk and sweep the mementos into a pile. Mum is working from home this morning. We are going to see the lawyer soon. Mum wants me to dress fairly smartly. By fairly smartly, she means a shirt and trousers.

*

The lawyer is sitting on the opposite side of the round table to me and Mum. We've been in here twenty minutes already, and all that's happened is the lawyer has explained what to expect at the trial. Mum has asked a load of questions. She has to leave soon as has a meeting at work. The lawyer places her elbows on the table and looks at me.

'Our job Horatio, is to make the jury sympathise with you.' She flicks a length of long brown hair off her forehead. 'Of course they will anyway, as you were attacked and left for dead. What we have to do, is to really get across to them, the jury, the trauma you experienced, and how it has affected you and your family. Do you understand?'

'Yes.'

Mum taps me twice on my left forearm. The lawyer says, 'One of the ways we can achieve this, is by you reading out a victim impact statement to the court. Now, I appreciate that must sound pretty daunting.'

'I've got no problem with it.'

Mum says, 'Good boy.'

The lawyer says, 'That's what I like to hear. The trial is still a little way off.' She presses the fingertips of both hands together. 'By perfecting what you are going to say in advance, it won't be too nerve-wracking when the day comes because you'll be well prepared.'

She explains this will be my chance for the court to hear my side of the story, and this is what we're going to be working on today. Mum gets up, says she has to leave for her meeting, tells me to do my best, to go straight home after I'm done, and that she should be home within two hours. Mum leaves. The lawyer picks up a pen. She asks me how the attack has affected me and what the emotional impact of it has been.

'I was in hospital and it has taken a while to recover. Still get a throbbing in my head sometimes.'

'Not surprising all things considered. It could be a lot worse.' She jots on a pad. 'And the emotional impact?'

Emotional, um ... 'I feel angry about it. Want Ra, him, to be locked up for a very long time. In a bad prison too. Not one of those cushy ones with golf courses they send rich people to. I want a dungeon.' She is giggling. 'One that practices medieval torture methods.' She giggles louder. *The rack. No, the best torture for rat would be rat torture. Ha!* 'Rat torture.'

She sits up straight – 'Excuse me?'

'Rat torture I said. Bind him to a table, put a rat in an upside-down bucket on his chest, and light a fire on the bucket. The rat can't get out so—'

‘Stop!’ She waves her hands in front of her face. She scrunches up her nose and doesn’t say anything for the best part of ten seconds. ‘It’s important not to express your anger, or state what you want to happen to him.’ Her eyes narrow. ‘Much as you might want to. Here’s an example statement.’ She picks up a piece of paper and reads from it. ‘Every morning when I wake up, I have to remind myself that my attacker can’t hurt me today. While I consider myself lucky to be alive, every day is a struggle.’

‘No way I’m saying that, makes me sound like a sissy.’

‘This isn’t about being macho. Don’t be scared to show your vulnerability.’ *Ah!* ‘Since being attacked, you’ve suffered from headaches, right?’

‘Yeah, sometimes I get them.’

‘How about this?’ She tilts her chin up. ‘Since being attacked by Roland Barstow. You’ll point at your attacker. I have suffered from anxiety and my confidence has been affected …’ *Yuck!* ‘Not a night goes by when I don’t get nightmares. All I wish for is my old life back. The life he …’ She looks at me … ‘took away.’ *Way too dweeby, there’s no way I’m saying it.* The lawyer puts the piece of paper down, leans forward and places her palms on the table. ‘You know everything you say to me is between us. It’s private, I won’t tell anyone. Client confidentiality is the term.’

‘Okay.’

‘Um, do you have any idea why he, Roland Barstow, might have attacked you? This could be important for your defence. I want to be prepared for every eventuality. Anything the prosecution might come up with.’ I nod. ‘So, this is how I understand it. Your attacker was best friends with your mother’s ex, who unfortunately passed away.’

‘That’s a strange way of putting it.’

‘What do you mean?’ She taps her fingertips on the desk. ‘I know he died; I know he died at home. From an accident your mother said.’

‘Yeah, it was an accident, an auto erotic asphyxiation accident. Accidentally strangled himself to death while jerking off to asphyxiation pornography.’ The lawyer’s mouth is hanging open. ‘He died in our living room. Had a belt around his neck, attached by a cord to the window. I saw him.’

*

The following Friday – This is the first time I have been to Serena’s house since the evening I became a serial killer. Mum told me yesterday I’m not grounded anymore. However, I have to be home by six-thirty *on the dot*. It’s four-fifty. Me and Serena have been in the park smoking skunk. We are now in her living room. Serena picks up a PlayStation controller.

‘This is the new *Street Fighter*. A friend lent it to me. Not normally into beat ’em ups, but this is badass. Ready to get your ass kicked?’

‘Never going to happen.’

‘Famous last words.’ She inserts the disk into the PlayStation. I dump myself on the sofa. Had three bongs in the park and am pretty stoned. My head is throbbing, but softly, and it’s not an unpleasant feeling. Serena collapses on the sofa next to me. ‘Battered.’ She hugs my neck and kisses me on the lips. I finger a length of her long, silky blonde hair. ‘My birthday isn’t far off.’ She blinks several times. ‘You know what that means, don’t you?’ I nod. Serena rubs the inside of my thigh. ‘Let’s do this.’

The new *Street Fighter* is pretty good. Serena’s character grabs me and judo throws me across the screen … My character is almost out of life. Serena attacks with a flurry of kicks, which I block. One more hit and I’m done. Her character is running at me from the other side of the screen. I crouch down, jump up and launch an uppercut to the underside of her character’s chin. She somersaults in the air and lands dead on the ground. That was the second-best uppercut I’ve ever thrown.

'Ha, ha haha.'

'What's so funny? You were so nearly dead there.' She slaps my leg. I get off the sofa and throw a right uppercut in the air. Then I do it again, and again. 'Stop doing that, it's getting boring.' I stop. 'Hungry?'

'Yeah.'

I've got the munchies. We go through to the kitchen. Serena gets Monster Munch from a cupboard and flicks a packet of roast beef flavour at me as if they were a frisbee. I catch them one handed.

'Your trial is coming up.'

'It's not my trial, it's Rat's. I'm innocent.'

'Innocent, you. *Hello.*' She puts a Monster Munch in her mouth and chews on it. 'How many weeks to go?'

'Three.'

'I'll be on holiday then with my grandparents in The Bahamas.' She is prodding at me with a Monster Munch. 'Rat hasn't got a leg to stand on. What is he going to say in court?'

ELEVEN

THREE WEEKS LATER – *Paleham Crown Court* – The judge is sitting behind a long table on a raised platform at the front of the courtroom. The twelve jurors are seated in a row diagonally behind her on burgundy-coloured chairs. My chair is the same colour; all the chairs here are. Mum and my sister are in the row behind me. I roll down the sleeve of the dark grey suit my father left me and check the time on the Swatch. 15:08.

When I lean forward and look to my left, I see Rat's long nose side-on. With a nose the length of Pinocchio's, there is no chance jurors are going to believe anything that comes out of his or his lawyer's mouth. He's not even wearing a suit, just a grey shirt and matching trousers, which are probably made of polyester. Not a surprise this, he wasn't wearing a suit for Fool's Gold's funeral. Rat's undersized head is shaved like a convict. Well, it's appropriate, he is a convict. He twists around and glares at me. Even from here, I can see the muscles bulging in the back of his gaunt cheeks. His lawyer is whispering in his ear. Rat twists around.

This morning, the trial kicked off with the court clerk reading out the charges. Attempted murder is the main one. It carries a maximum life term. Rat is in deep shit. Serves the loser right for attacking me. Would rather kill him and take a memento than he get sent to jail. But life imprisonment isn't bad, as second prizes go. Earlier this afternoon, the jury were shown CCTV footage of

Rat before and after the attack. Had already seen the grainy clip of him on the street wearing a hood before the attack. In the post-attack footage, Rat is sprinting along the pavement of a main road with his tool bag slung over his shoulder. The footage is grainy too. But everyone in the court could clearly see the man with the exceedingly long nose was running away.

My lawyer has already called up two witnesses to the stand. Passers-by who saw Rat fleeing after he attacked me. Both pointed him out without hesitation. When they did, Rat curled his fingers. Now it's the turn of the star witness, the woman who was putting the rubbish out when Rat was attacking me. She strides over to the stand. My lawyer asks her to identify the person who attacked me. She points at Rat and states he was the man she saw brandishing a hammer on the other side of the street, when she was putting the rubbish out. Rat is gripping the arms of his chair. The witness says she raced out of her front gate into the street and got a good look at his face, as he was lit up by a streetlight and the hood he was wearing had fallen off.

Problems are mounting for Rat, one on top of the other. The judge will be aware he is a convicted criminal. When it comes to sentencing, she'll jail him for the longest time possible. A life sentence with a minimum term of fifteen or twenty years is what my lawyer thinks. She is talking now. Does a lot of talking this lawyer. There's no need, this is a done deal. But this is the way trials play out, it seems. Keeps people in jobs I suppose.

While she drones on, I peer up at the ceiling and remember the time Rat was arrested by the police in the cemetery at Fool's Gold's burial. I took Aunt Fatso's phone from her handbag, phoned the police from behind a gravestone, and told them Rat was trying to abuse the children of some of the funeral guests. When they came and arrested him, I watched from a bench. Rat assumed it was no big deal because he thought they were there as he'd been smoking weed in the cemetery. But then the police searched his record bag and found the erotic asphyxiation paraphernalia I had planted. Brightly coloured sashes tied as nooses and erotic asphyxiation pornographic pictures I'd printed off the internet.

'Ha, haha.'

My lawyer nudges me with her elbow. I put my forearm over my mouth to stop myself laughing. Would have been really embarrassing for Rat. He went to prison for it. Though can't have been for long, as he was out by the time I returned from Antigua. Guess there wasn't enough evidence he was trying to throttle children in the cemetery. They assumed he was a sicko and put him in prison for a short while. He'll be on the sex offender register. And the judge must know he's on it. Every time she looks at Rat, the corners of her mouth curl down.

Rat doesn't have a leg to stand on, as there is no way his lawyer can claim he didn't do it. He is pleading guilty and going to claim diminished responsibility. It's all the loser can do. There's a saying for the position he's got himself in – stuck between a rock and a hard place. Why does the trial have to take so long when everyone knows he did it? Has to be proven to the jury it happened is one reason. When it is time for the defence, Rat's lawyer is going to try and make excuses for him. Wonder what they will be. He can't try to claim I killed his best friend and planted erotic asphyxiation paraphernalia on him. There's no proof; it sounds ridiculous. No one will believe him because he's a criminal anyway. Also, regardless, it doesn't mean he's allowed to try and kill me with a hammer. His lawyer is going to claim he was delusional and is mentally ill. All it will result in, is Rat swapping prison for the nuthouse.

'Haha.'

I put my forearm over my mouth. When the session ends, I go home on the tube with Mum and my sister. On the journey, they whisper to each other about the trial. When we get home, Mum says we need a break, and we should forget the trial until tomorrow. For dinner, we order pizza.

*

13:07 – The next day – My lawyer is holding up a transparent plastic bag with a hammer in it. The hammer he attacked me with. The moron dropped it in a bin when he was running away, and the police found it. My blood and Rat's fingerprints were on the hammer. Was in a such a panic, he forgot to wipe them off. My lawyer tells the court this is the weapon Roland Barstow tried to kill me with. When she finishes, it will be my turn to make my victim impact statement. Got it memorised. My lawyer says it's *powerful stuff* and will have quite an effect on the jury. I reach into my suit jacket's left side pocket, unravel the tissue in it and finger the gold-capped molar I brought to court with me today. Occurred to me last night it would be a good idea to bring the tooth, as it reminds me of my first kill, Rat's best friend, and surely only friend, Fool's Gold.

At breakfast today, Mum said she couldn't stop wondering *what that horrible man's excuse* will be for attacking me. *None of it makes sense* she said. Rat's lawyer will claim he's mad. Guess he is mad in a way, otherwise he would never have attacked me. Rat was never going to get away with it … My lawyer has stopped talking. It is time for me to deliver my victim impact statement. This is my moment to shine. I take a deep inhalation through my nose and stand up. Everyone is looking at me.

'I was returning from boxing training when you …' I fix my gaze on Rat, … 'crept up behind me.' Rat has lifted his upper lip and is displaying a yellow incisor. The jury are going to love that. 'You attacked me with frenzied and repeated blows to the head with a hammer. And you only stopped when you were scared off by Francesca, who came out of her house and challenged you. At which point you fled in the same cowardly fashion you attacked me.' Rat's muttering something. 'I was rushed to hospital, where I endured an operation and multi-day stay.'

Multi-days sounds better than two. 'Due to the injuries you inflicted, I have suffered from severe migraines and recurring nightmares.' *Have only had three nightmares. This is what my lawyer calls an embellishment.* 'I still suffer from the injuries I sustained from you.' Rat is trembling. 'However ...' I hold my right index finger up. 'Today, I feel stronger, more alive, and more determined to fulfil my potential than ever. While the physical and mental scars will always be with me, you have not taken away my will to live, my will to succeed. You are a cowardly criminal.' *The next bit's my favourite.* 'A stain on society.' So violently is Rat shaking, it's as if his chair has transformed into an electric chair. 'I refuse to be a victim—'

'CUNT!'

Rat. The judge brings her gavel down, and bellows, 'You are in contempt of court. Court security remove him!'

I hear my sister say, 'Oh my God.'

Two uniformed men approach Rat, grip onto his arms and haul him away.

'Get off me!'

Rat is going to miss the end of my victim impact statement. Will have to change it now, as I'm not addressing him directly.

'His cowardly attack will not dictate my future.' I fix my eyes on the jury. 'My family and I put our faith in you, the jury, to dispense justice and to protect society from this vile and cowardly predator ... Thank you.'

My lawyer says, 'Good job.'

Mum murmurs, 'Well done.'

I sit down. It was some performance; the jury are impressed. One of them is nodding. The *putting faith* part was a bit soppy. But my lawyer insisted on it. Presently, she is summing up. While she speaks, I unwrap the tissue in the side pocket of my blazer and feel the gold-capped molar. Would have brought the gold chain and medallion with me today. However, we get searched coming in, and Mum and my sister would want to know where I had got it, and why I had it with me.

*

12:51 – The following afternoon – Rat's back. This morning the judge warned him about his conduct. Hasn't been a squeak out of him since. Has been snarling a fair bit though and showing his yellow incisor. Rat evidently hasn't been to the dentist in years. He is glaring at me. Been doing a fair bit of this too. It's the defence's turn today. So far, it has been a joke. And the joke is on Rat. His lawyer is attempting to blame the attack on *extenuating factors*. He is claiming Rat didn't actually intend to try and kill me. It isn't going to wash.

'Rollie had a challenging upbringing. An absent father, an alcoholic mother, several stints in care homes … Rollie's psychological state was severely affected by the unfortunate and premature death of his best friend, Brandon …' *There was nothing unfortunate about it. And it wasn't premature; it was overdue.* 'Brandon was Horatio Robinson's mother's partner.'

Rat is snarling again. Reckon he wanted his lawyer to try and blame the attack on me killing his best friend. But his lawyer would have refused, saying it was ridiculous, and the jury wouldn't buy it. Minimising responsibility is all he's got to run with.

'This was not a pre-meditated attack.' *Bullshit.* 'Rollie had no intention of hurting anyone.' *Premeditated is worse than spur of the moment is why his lawyer's spewing this rubbish.* 'Rollie was in a pub after work drinking … Unfortunately, he has been afflicted by mental health issues, which have been exacerbated by drinking and smoking marijuana.' *He used to do drugs at my house. Thought it was cool. It's not. Not when you're near-on forty and a complete loser.* 'This abnormality of mental functioning substantially impaired his decision making … He was suffering from paranoia, and in his altered state was irrationally blaming the Robinson family for the death of his best friend. This is why he acted in such an uncharacteristic way … It was a moment of madness.'

Rat is gripping onto the sides of his chair. He must be clenching down hard with his yellow teeth because the muscles are bulging in the backs of his cheeks. My lawyer nudges me and says out of the side of her mouth, 'Stop looking at him.'

I twist my head ninety degrees and look straight ahead. His lawyer is droning on about diminished responsibility and how Rat didn't intend to kill me. He claims his judgement was clouded and he is not a violent man. The lawyer shows the court letters from doctors, stating that Rat has mental health problems. Basically, what the lawyer is saying, is he should have been euthanised at birth. Finally, he finishes. Rat isn't going to say anything then. Suits me just fine, as don't want him throwing accusations at me. It's not as if the jury or anyone else is going to believe him. Preferable though if he keeps his mouth shut.

My lawyer makes a closing speech, asking for justice for me and my family. And then Rat's lawyer makes a short speech that predictably tries to reduce the idiot's responsibility, by reason of being a complete loser. When his lawyer says how remorseful *Rollie is*, Rat's face turns bright red. The judge is summing up … She's done. The jurors leave the courtroom. Shouldn't take them long to reach the right verdict – guilty of attempted murder. It better not take them long, as it's 15:03 now, and I don't want to have to return tomorrow.

Me, Mum and my sister go to a nearby café. They order cappuccinos and caramel slices. I get a Coca-Cola and a chocolate brownie. They chat virtually non-stop to each other about the trial. Quietly though, so no one at the other tables can hear. Mum says she is expecting the severest sentence possible, which is life. My sister thinks because of the lawyer's claims about Rat's mental health, there will be further assessments, and sentencing will be deferred to a later date. What is certain, is the judge is going to throw the book at Rat. He will probably be in jail for decades.

'Haha.'

They are looking at me. I have a bite of chocolate brownie;

they continue talking. Mum is saying Rat's reason for attempting to kill me, a moment of madness, is completely illogical. My sister says Rollie is demented, couldn't think straight, and that's all there is to it. Mum says even if that was the case, it doesn't add up. My phone beeps. Phones aren't allowed in court. I collected it on the way out and will hand it back when we return. It's a text from Serena, asking if the trial is over yet and what happened. I will text her when it's over. The jury shouldn't be deliberating for much longer.

We return to the court and wait in the foyer. It's 16:11. *Hurry up!* There is no need for this delay. The jury are probably taking the opportunity to have a tea break. Or maybe they think it makes them look professional if they take their time ... Twelve minutes have passed, and we are still waiting. Mum is nibbling her fingernails again. I look up at the ceiling. My lawyer comes over and speaks to us ... The door to the courtroom opens and a staff member tells us to come inside. We go in and take our seats. Rat is already here. He is leaning forward in his chair, expanding and deflating his cheeks. When I look at him, he snarls and raises his fist. *Ha* he might as well be dead; his life is over. My lawyer tugs on my sleeve. I stop looking at Rat.

Where are the jury? Been in here five minutes and they still haven't appeared. Behind me, I hear Mum breathing heavily and my sister muttering something. The jury come through a side entrance in a line, some of them with their heads bowed, others looking straight ahead. Leading the way is an old man. He is the foreperson. The foreperson is the first person selected as a juror. The judge asks, 'Has the jury reached a verdict?'

'Yes,' says the foreperson. He is holding an envelope, which he takes ages opening. He pulls a piece of paper from it, and coughs, 'A-ha.' There is a pause. Here goes. 'We, the jury, find the defendant Roland Barstow guilty of attempted murder.'

Perfect. My lawyer is smiling at me. Rat's head has gone bright red. I hear Mum say, 'Phew.'

The judge says, 'Sentencing is adjourned until mental health assessments have been conduct—'

'MURDERER!'

Rat leaps off his seat and charges towards me. I stand up and raise my fists to my chin. My lawyer is shrieking, so is my sister. His lawyer is pursuing him. Rat is two metres away from me when his lawyer rugby tackles him. Rat hasn't uttered a word the entire trial, and now this. The judge brings her gavel down.

'You are in contempt of court.'

'Fucking know you did it!'

Rat squirms his ankles free from his lawyer's grip and clambers to his feet. I shuffle back and prepare to hit him with a right cross to the tip of his long nose. Two court security men are racing this way. Rat has spotted them. He lurches away and scuttles around the front row of seats towards Mum. Rat drops to his knees in front of her, presses his palms together, and screeches, 'Your son killed Brandon!' The judge is hammering away with the gavel. 'Please believe me, I'm not a bad person.' Mum's mouth is hanging open and my sister's hands are on her head. 'Think about it. Brandon wasn't into erotic asphyxiation, swear to God. And Horatio was the only person in the house.'

Mum slaps Rat's cheek. Nice. The judge bellows, 'Take him away!'

One of the court security grabs Rat by the ankles and drags him away from Mum. He is clawing at the floor, the judge is banging her gavel, my sister is tugging her hair, Mum is biting her lower lip, and Rat is screaming, 'Was a set-up. Fucking obvious! The police found erotic asphyxiation shit in my bag at the cemetery. Didn't know that, did yah?' He is dragged out of the aisle. 'Nooses 'n that. Why would I be carrying them about, eh?' The other security man grabs his arms. 'Horatio changed the funeral music. How else could it have been changed to *Take Your Breath Away*?' He is lifted up by his arms and legs. 'Chances are one in a billion.' Rat is carried away squirming and screeching.

'Erotic asphyxiation came out the blue and it was suddenly fucking everywhere. Brandon, the song, me!' *Get him out of here.* He's nearly at the exit. 'Rakesha, think! Horatio, you sick murdering fuck!' He is being carried through the door. 'DEVIL *CUNT*!'

Rat's gone. Everyone is looking at each other. My lawyer is staring at me. When I look at her, she gulps and looks away. Mum mutters, 'Oh my God.'

My sister is clinging onto her arm. The jury are trotting off. Some of them have twisted their heads and are looking in my direction. I follow Mum and my sister out of the courtroom. In the foyer, my lawyer says goodbye to Mum, blurts 'Bye' to me, and scuttles off.

On the tube, when I sit next to my sister, she shifts to the far side of her seat and tilts towards Mum. Neither of them says much on the journey, and they don't utter a word to me. Has been a while since I thought about changing Fool's Gold's funeral song from *Never Say Goodbye* by Bon Jovi to the theme tune for *Top Gun, Take My Breath Away.* Was hilarious. Rat went berserk, as did Fool's Gold's father. Can hear the lyrics in my head.

Watching every motion in my foolish lover's game
On this endless ocean, finally lovers know no shame
Turning and returning to some secret place inside
Watching in slow motion as you turn around and say
Take my breath away
Take my breath away

'Ha!'

I bite the sleeve of my suit jacket to stop myself laughing aloud. My eyes are watering. I clamp down harder with my teeth. I need to replace the lyrics in my head with something serious. Maths, physics, equations ... *Take my breath away* ... Maths, physics, equations. Maths, physics, equations ... That did the trick. I stop biting the sleeve and put my arm down by my side. No one is going to believe Rat. He is a convicted criminal and an absolute loser. Considering how Fool's Gold died, it was unlikely the song was changed accidentally to *Take My Breath Away*. But who's to say I did it?

*

Since getting home, I have been in my room. Spent time with my mementos, used the algebra app on my phone, and done some reading. No one has bothered me. Thought maybe Mum might want to celebrate. Crack open the champagne and tuck into some hors d'oeuvres. Hasn't happened though, not yet anyway. Guess it's because Mum was expecting Rat to be found guilty, so it wasn't a big surprise when he was. Currently, I'm lying on my bed peering up at the ceiling and fingering the gold medallion hanging from the chain around my neck. Would have knocked Rat out if his lawyer hadn't rugby tackled him. The good news is prison will be bad for Rat. He's no badass gangster type and will be picked on. The bad news is Rat won't have to worry about picking the soap up off the floor in the showers. Rat is rank, and no prisoner will want to get it on with him. Unless there's a rat fetishist prisoner.

'HAHA!' My phone is ringing. It's Serena, phoning from The Bahamas. I never did text her. 'Hello.'

'Hey. What happened? Did they find him guilty?'

'Sure did.'

She squeals, 'Awesome.' Sounds like she is clapping her hands. 'How long is Rat going to jail for? Hope it's forever.'

'Sentencing is adjourned.'

'Adjourned? Um, means it will happen later, right?'

'Yeah.'

'Oh, pity.'

'Yes, it is. He's been done for attempted murder though, so he will be locked up for a long time. At least a decade. Should be more.'

'Cool. You'll go to the sentencing?'

'Yeah, probably. Imagine Mum will want to be there for it.'

'Bet your Mum is really happy now he's been found guilty.'

When I finish the call, it's gone eight o'clock. Why hasn't Mum called me for dinner? I go downstairs. The kitchen door is closed. It rarely is. What're they talking about in there? I tiptoe up to the door and press my ear to it. Can hear them talking, but not the words. Previously, when I've listened in on conversations from out here, I've been able to hear what's being said. They must be talking quietly. I open the door. They are pressed together at the kitchen table. They pull their chairs apart. I step into the room.

'What's for dinner?'

Mum mumbles, 'Haven't decided yet.'

'It's gone eight.' I open the fridge. Not much in here apart from eggs and vegetables. Mum forgot to get food on the way back. In a cupboard there are some noodles. Could have these as a last resort. But I would prefer takeaway. 'Mum?' She sighs. 'There's virtually no food. We should get takeaway.' Mum murmurs something I can't hear. 'Takeaway, I said. Pizza again.'

Mum says, 'No.'

'Come on, to celebrate. Shaneeka, you must want pizza?'

My sister doesn't reply. They're not even looking at me. Noodles it is then. I go over to the cupboard and pull them out. When I turn around, they are gone.

TWELVE

15:08 – THE FOLLOWING SATURDAY – I'm on my way home from the boxing gym. Haven't been up to much since the trial. Reading, studying, watching television, hanging out with my mementos. That's about it. Had the house to myself most of the time, which has been good. Mum has been at work a lot, every day this week. Usually, she works from home two days a week. Probably has meetings is why she's been there so much. My sister isn't at home this weekend for once. Am planning to go to Serena's later. She's back from The Bahamas. Her birthday is next week; she's having a party at her friend's house.

I turn the key in the front door and push it open. Mum is standing in the entrance to the living room. This is the third time this week I've caught her doing it. She swivels around and sighs. I close the door, and say, 'Planning to go to Serena's this evening.' She rotates her head and peers into the living room. 'Were you listening? I'm going to Serena's later.'

'Yeah, sure.' Mum is going upstairs. 'There's something for you in your room on your desk.'

What could it be? I go into the kitchen and shove my sweaty gym clothes in the washing machine, then head upstairs to my room. I drop the gym bag on the floor and walk over to the desk. On the desk, there are two magazines. No, they are not magazines, they are school prospectuses. This is promising. I pick them up. They are prospectuses for boarding schools. Boarding schools a long way from London. One is in Northumberland; that's near Scotland. The other is in Yorkshire. Yorkshire is not a million miles from Scotland either. I flick through the prospectuses. Amazing these schools look, nothing like the shithole I go to. They have playing fields, libraries, art centres, science centres. The school in Northumberland has a chapel practically the size of a cathedral. It even has stained glass windows. There will be no Dunces in these schools, and no school gangs. So, Mum has taken on board what I said for once and is planning to send me to a new school. I clap my hands. Excellent news this.

Better to be on the other side of the country than at my present school, that's for sure. Earlier this week, Tuesday it was, heard Mum talking to an estate agent on the phone. She's changed her mind and is going to sell Aunt Fatso's flat, not rent it out. I tap my chin with my right index finger. This must be how she is planning to pay the fees. Boarding schools cost a fortune. I will go and talk to Mum about these schools.

But first I will spend a minute or two with my mementos. I reach under the chest of drawers, remove the tape securing the fly-fishing tin to it, sit on my bed, open the fly-fishing tin, examine the contents, and remove the monocle. Wonder how my father came by this old-fashioned monocle. A teacher might be sporting a monocle at my new boarding school.

To be continued in 2025.